Michelle & Debra

Michelle & Debra

JACK WEYLAND

Deseret Book Company
Salt Lake City

Library of Congress Cataloging-in-Publication Data

Weyland, Jack, 1940–
    Michelle and Debra / by Jack Weyland.
        p. cm.
    Summary: Michelle and Debra, Mormons and best friends, see their lives diverging at the end of their teen years, as Michelle meets and decides to marry a boy who follows the standards of their church while Debra must deal with the many times she has violated its teachings on chastity.
    ISBN 0-87579-369-X
    [1. Sexual ethics — Fiction.   2. Mormons — Fiction.   3. Christian life — Fiction.] I. Title.
PZ7.W538Mi   1990
[Fic] — dc20
                                       90-3647
                                          CIP
                                           AC

Printed in the United States of America

10   9   8   7   6   5   4

Other Books by Jack Weyland

Novels
Charly
Sam
The Reunion
PepperTide
A New Dawn
The Understudy
Last of the Big-time Spenders
Sara, Whenever I Hear Your Name
Brenda at the Prom
Stephanie

Short Stories
A Small Light in the Darkness
Punch and Cookies Forever
First Day of Forever

Nonfiction
If Talent Were Pizza, You'd Be a Supreme

1

When Michelle was thirteen, she made a decision that affected the rest of her life. Seven years later, on August 24, 1990, she was married in the temple.

Debra, her best friend, wasn't quite sure what she wanted from life. At first she was willing to live the way the Church teaches, but as time passed she found it too restrictive. For Debra at thirteen it was indecision that left her vulnerable to what happened later in her life.

This is their story.

June 1983: Michelle and Debra at Thirteen

For Michelle Raner and Debra Cassidy, being thirteen was a time of grand adventure, not the least of which was girls' camp. Even had Sister Drummond, the camp director, assigned them different tents, they would have talked someone into changing just so they could be together. They had been together since the first grade, when Debra's family had moved next door to Michelle's family in Salt Lake City.

At thirteen they were both so determined to be different that they were the same. Even so, there were some noticeable differences between them.

Michelle was the fourth child in a family of five children. Her father's parents had emigrated from Yugoslavia when he was just a baby. Michelle had inherited his dark complexion; year-around she looked the way her friends could look only in July and August after weeks of lying in the sun. She had long, dark brown hair and thick, bushy eyebrows, which gave drama and mystery to even the most innocent of her expressions.

Debra was the youngest of six children. She came after her parents thought they were through raising kids. Her next oldest brother was eight years older, so at thirteen she was the only child still at home. In grade school she dreaded the times when parents were invited to school because her parents always looked so old. She had long blond hair and blue eyes accented by heavy, dark eye shadow. Her parents told her it made her look as if she had been hit with a baseball bat, but she didn't pay much attention to their opinions. She had a way of looking at people that made them think she was skeptical of what they said, but it wasn't skepticism so much as it was that she needed glasses but refused to wear them.

At girls' camp that year Michelle and Debra were assigned to the same tent, which they would share with Angela McPherson. As soon as they arrived, Angela sprayed an entire can of bug repellent around the area where they were to pitch their tent.

"But, Angela, the outdoors is the bugs' home," Michelle observed.

"Not anymore it isn't," Angela said grimly, as she left to borrow another can of repellent.

Debra turned to Michelle. "Okay, when do we put a frog in her sleeping bag?"

"As soon as you catch the frog."

"Why do I have to be the one who catches the frog?"

"Because it's your idea. Look, help me get this tent up. I shouldn't have to do everything."

"What do you want me to do?" Debra asked.

"I don't know. Do something."

2

Debra punched her arm.

"Knock it off."

"You said to do something. Hitting you is doing something."

"You're not going to help me at all, are you?"

"Help you do what? Stand around? Because that's all you're doing. You think if you look helpless long enough, Sister Drummond will come and put the tent up for us, right?"

"I can put it up."

"Then put it up."

"I will . . . just as soon as I figure out what all these poles are for."

"They're to hold the tent up."

"Gosh, thanks, like I never would've thought of that by myself."

"Hey, glad to help out."

Eventually Sister Drummond came and helped put the tent up.

That night after group prayer they went to their tent. Debra wasn't sleepy. "Let's go toilet-paper the mess hall."

"We'll do that our last night," Michelle said.

"Will you two be quiet so I can sleep?" Angela complained.

"Sleep?" Debra said. "You think we came here to sleep? We can sleep anytime. Right now let's talk about boys." She leaned in Angela's direction and said in a deep voice, "I've never seen you look more lovely than you do tonight, my dear." She kissed her own hand, making it sound loud and slobbery.

Michelle started to laugh.

Angela wasn't amused. "Quit messing around, Debra. We're supposed to be sleeping now."

"Why? Nobody else is," Debra said.

"Yes they are."

Debra called out in a loud voice, "Hey, is anybody out there sleeping yet? Angela wants to know."

"You girls quiet down!" Sister Drummond called out.

Debra waited about ten seconds and then began speaking softly again. "Okay, now let's talk about boys."

"Is that all you can think of?" Angela asked.

"All right, let's talk about what a fine clarinet player Angela is becoming. Angela, I do hope you brought your clarinet with you and that you'll play us all a solo. We all enjoy hearing you play the same song every week at Young Women's."

There was a long pause. "I only played my clarinet at Young Women's one time, Debra."

Debra realized Angela had been hurt, so she tried to make it better. "And it was really good, too. I'm serious. I went home and told my parents how good you played. Isn't that right, Michelle, didn't Angela do a good job?"

"Yes, real good."

"I've got an idea," Debra said. "Let's all go down to the dock. That way we can talk as much as we want without bothering anybody."

"We're not supposed to go down there unless there's a lifeguard on duty," Angela said.

"Oh sure, like it's so dangerous down there ... like we'd be down there and this huge sea monster would come and swallow us whole. C'mon, you guys, let's go."

"Not me," Angela said.

"Michelle then. C'mon."

Michelle crawled out of her sleeping bag. "We won't be gone long," she told Angela as she and Debra got dressed.

Debra started to leave the tent, then poked her head back in. "It's dark out here. Get a flashlight." She went back outside.

"I don't see why you do whatever she says," Angela said to Michelle, who was still putting on her boots.

"We're best friends. Haven't you ever had a best friend?"

"Once ... but she moved."

Michelle rummaged around. "Have you seen my flashlight?"

"You can use mine," Angela said.

4

"Thanks. Are you sure you don't want to come with us?"

"Before we came here we promised to obey the rules of the camp. I think that's what we should do."

"I agree with that."

"Then why are you going?" She held out her flashlight.

Michelle thought a moment, then said, "You remember Sister Drummond talking about the buddy system? How we're supposed to stay together when we go anyplace? Well, if I don't go with Debra now, then she'll go alone, but if I go with her, then it'll be safer for her. 'Bye." She crawled out of the tent and joined Debra.

"I'm hungry," Debra whispered. "Let's go to the commissary. When I was on KP today, I unlocked one of the windows. C'mon."

At the commissary, Debra went through the open window and then let Michelle in.

"Bring the flashlight over here," Debra said.

They found several boxes of candy bars.

"Help yourself," Debra said.

"We shouldn't be doing this," Michelle said.

"Why not? We helped pay for the food at camp, didn't we?"

"Yes."

"Then that means it's ours, right? Which means it's okay for us to have some."

Michelle hesitated, then took a candy bar. "Well, okay, but when they pass out candy bars, I won't take one because I'll already have had mine."

"Yeah, right." Debra grabbed three of the bars and then rearranged the rest to make the box look full. "Let's go."

Once they got to the lake, they sat at the end of the dock and ate. "Everybody should be down here instead of stuck in a tent," Debra said.

"Look at how many stars you can see tonight." Michelle lay on her back and looked up at the sky. "Makes you think about God, doesn't it?"

"I suppose." Debra opened a candy bar and took a bite. "What would you do if you found out there's no God so it didn't really matter what you did?"

Michelle thought about it. "Some things are wrong whether there's a God or not."

"Like what?"

"Well, like killing, for example."

"Okay, we won't kill anyone. Anything else?"

"Anything that hurts somebody else is wrong."

"What about sex?" Debra asked, taking a big bite of a candy bar.

"What about it?"

"Are you going to wait until you get married?"

"I guess so. What about you?"

"I'm not sure. My mom and dad say that's the best way. But sometimes I'm not so sure. I mean, after all, they also like the taste of asparagus. So maybe they're wrong about the other too." She paused. "Just kidding. I'll probably wait too."

"Sometimes I think about the person I'm going to marry," Michelle mused. "Like on a night like this I think that maybe he's outside right this minute looking at the stars and thinking about me too."

Debra acted as if she was in a trance. "You're right, I can see him now. He's out walking along a highway, looking up at the stars, thinking about you. Oh, no! Look out! Look out!"

"What?"

"There's a big truck coming down the highway. It's going too fast. The driver doesn't see him on the highway. Oh, no! What a terrible accident! Sorry, Michelle, but the guy you were going to marry just got wasted. Too bad."

"You're crazy. You know that, don't you?"

"Yeah, but in a nice way, right?"

"Yeah, most of the time." Michelle paused. "When I get married, I think I'd like it to be in the Salt Lake Temple."

"When did you decide that?"

"One time when I was little, our family went to Temple Square to see the Christmas lights. I was cold and sleepy and my dad picked me up and carried me around, but I started fussing so he goes, 'Michelle, look around. This is where you're going to be married someday.' For some reason that stuck with me."

"Who wants to think about that now?" Debra looked around. "Hey, I've got an idea—let's go canoeing."

"We're not supposed to unless there's a lifeguard on duty."

"Don't turn into another Angela on me, okay?"

"But what if we get caught?"

"We won't get caught."

They dragged a canoe into the water and paddled out to the middle of the small lake.

Debra started mimicking Sister Drummond. "Young lady, where's your life jacket? What, you don't have a life jacket? Young lady, what would I tell your parents if you drowned? These rules are for your own safety. This is not time to have fun—we will tell you when it's time to have fun."

Michelle started laughing. "You sound just like her."

"I have more fun with you than anybody else." Debra quit paddling. "No matter what, let's promise we'll always stay best friends. Okay?"

Michelle was surprised Debra was so serious. "Okay, sure."

"Like . . . let's make like this solemn pledge that no matter what, we'll always look out for each other. It'll be like a buddy system that goes on forever. Okay? Say it."

"I promise I'll always be your buddy and help you out whenever you need me," Michelle said.

"I promise I'll do the same for you." There was a long silence. "Don't ever forget, okay?"

"I won't."

"Okay." Suddenly Debra got a mischievous look on her face. "Like even if the wind came up . . ."—she grabbed the sides of the canoe and started rocking it—". . . we'd still stick together. Even if the canoe tipped over, we'd both drown together."

Michelle held on. She wanted to laugh but was afraid the noise would wake everybody up, so she had to hold it back, but that made her want to laugh even more. Finally she couldn't help it any longer. They both started laughing, and they couldn't seem to stop.

"Who's down there in the canoe?" a voice rang out.

"Let's get out of here," Debra said. While Sister Drummond made her way down the trail to the lake, the two girls paddled as fast as they could to the opposite side. They found a place protected by trees from Sister Drummond's view, beached the canoe, then ran through the trees back toward camp. A short time later they slipped into their tent and climbed into their sleeping bags.

Suddenly they heard voices. It was Sister Drummond waking up the other leaders. "Two of the girls were out in a canoe. Please check each tent and tell me who's missing."

A minute later someone opened the flap of Michelle and Debra's tent and shined a flashlight around. They pretended to be asleep. The leader moved to the next tent.

Much later they heard one of the women saying, "There's no one missing."

"Are you sure Debra is in her tent? She can be kind of mischievous at times," another voice said.

"Yes, I checked. You say you saw two people in a canoe?"

"Yes."

"Even if it was Debra, who'd be the other girl? Michelle is her best friend."

"Oh, Michelle wouldn't do anything like that."

Debra leaned over and whispered, mimicking the adult voice, "Oh, Michelle wouldn't do anything like that."

Michelle poked Debra in the side.

"Maybe it wasn't any of our girls," Sister Drummond said.

"Maybe it was just a couple of fishermen, except it sounded like two girls giggling."

"We can question everyone in the morning. Let's go get some sleep."

In the tent Angela, who they thought had been asleep, broke the silence. "I told you not to go. You should have listened to me."

"You're not going to tell on us, are you?" Debra asked.

"I guess not. Where's my flashlight?"

"We must have left it in the canoe," Michelle said. "We'll get it first thing in the morning."

"I need it now."

"Why?"

"I might have to get up in the middle of the night."

Michelle started to get out of her sleeping bag.

"I'll get it," Debra said.

"Thanks."

"No problem." She crawled out of the tent.

"I wish I wasn't in a tent with the two of you," Angela said after Debra had gone.

"Why?" Michelle asked.

"All week it's going to be you and her together and me on the outside. I'm tired of being the one people can't decide what to do with." She paused. "Like when my brother died. Everybody wishes it had been me instead of Troy."

"Why should they think that?"

"Because he was so good at sports. They all say he'd have made All State in football this year. The only thing I'm good at is the clarinet—but nobody cares if you're good at the clarinet." She paused. "Sometimes I feel so alone. I wish I had a friend . . . like you have Debra."

"You and I are friends."

"It's not the same."

"No, but maybe it can be sometime."

"Yeah, maybe."

9

They didn't talk anymore. A while later Debra came in the tent. "Here's your flashlight, Angela." She got ready for bed and slipped into her sleeping bag. Angela took the flashlight and left the tent.

"Let's lock her in the restroom," Debra whispered.

"No, we can't do anything more tonight."

There was a long pause. "So . . . *when* will we lock Angela in the restroom?"

Michelle ignored the question and turned away from Debra so she'd know it was time to sleep.

The next morning at flag ceremony Sister Drummond announced, "I saw two girls in a canoe last night. I need to know who it was."

Nobody volunteered any information. There was nothing else to do but to talk about the importance of rules and then move on to other things. She announced that during the week each girl was expected to spend one hour in nature study. She offered a pair of binoculars for the girls to use, as she put it, to study the local flora and fauna.

After breakfast, Debra took a walk alone. Half an hour later she came back. "C'mon, Michelle, let's get Sister Drummond's binoculars. Hurry, before the wildlife I saw moves."

"You saw some wildlife?"

"Yeah. C'mon, hurry."

When Michelle and Debra asked to borrow the binoculars, Sister Drummond was pleased that Debra was finally taking an interest in camp activities. She gave the girls a notebook and a pencil to record their observations.

Debra led the way. They crossed two fences and ended up on a ridge overlooking a farmhouse. Two boys were bent over a car, trying to fix something.

"Now that's my kind of wildlife," Debra said. "They do look kind of wild, don't they?"

Michelle smiled. "That's not what Sister Drummond had in mind."

"Well, maybe not, but answer me this, are those two creatures in the woods?"

"No."

"But if the farmhouse wasn't there, would they be in the woods?"

"I guess so."

"Are they both a part of nature?"

"No."

"Wrong. You're a part of nature, I'm a part of nature, everything is a part of nature. Those guys are also a part of nature. So let's observe them." She put the binoculars to her eyes.

"Okay, but I get to have some time observing too."

"Sure, that's only fair." Debra looked through the binoculars. "The creatures are both healthy specimens. Write that down."

Michelle grabbed for the binoculars. "Let me see."

"No, get away. You'll have your chance later."

"When?"

"How about if I watch for five minutes and then you watch for five minutes. That way it'll be fair."

They watched for a while, then Debra said, "Let's go talk to the creatures."

"No."

"Why not? It's either talk to those guys or else stay and watch Angela spray the tent again with bug spray. Which would you rather do?"

Led by Debra, they sauntered into the farmyard. "Hi, guys. How's it going?"

"Where'd you two come from?" one of the boys asked.

"From outer space," Debra said. "This here is Vulcan and I'm Larvana. Our space ship just broke down."

"Yeah, right."

"It's true."

They talked for an hour. They all gave each other made-up names and lied about their ages.

"You two want to do something tonight?" one of the boys asked.

"Like what?"

"I don't know. We could go for a ride or something."

"We'd better stick around camp," Michelle said. "The other girl in our tent will tell on us if we're gone very long."

"How about if we meet you at the dock by the lake at eleven o'clock tonight?"

"Okay," Debra said.

A minute later they were walking back to camp. "We're not really going to meet 'em, are we?" Michelle said.

"Sure, why not?"

"What if we get caught?"

"We won't get caught."

"That's what you said last night."

"We didn't get caught, did we?"

"C'mon, Debra, this is supposed to be a girls' camp."

"I know. Pretty boring, right?"

"Look, I really don't think this is a good idea. We don't even know them."

"That's why we're meeting them, so we can get to know 'em."

"Besides, they're not all that great," Michelle said.

"I know that, but look, they're the best we can do here. It's like Sister Drummond says: out in the woods you have to learn to make do."

That night at supper they had gingersnaps for dessert. Someone must have got a good deal on them because they were as hard as rocks, and eating one sounded like a rock crusher at work. Most of the girls didn't like them, but Debra did. She ended up with almost a full box. All during the program around the campfire, she continued to eat them until finally Angela couldn't stand it. "Quit making so much noise!"

"It's not me, it's the gingersnaps."

"Well, quit eating them then."

"Okay, okay. I just don't see why you get so mad about everything."

After the campfire program, just after the three girls crawled into their sleeping bags, there was silence until Debra said, "Please pass the gingersnaps."

That set Angela off. "That's it. I want out of here."

"I was just kidding, okay? Actually I'm pretty sleepy tonight." She yawned. "How about you, Michelle?"

"Yeah, I'm sleepy too."

"Nighty-night, Angela. Don't let the bedbugs bite," Debra said.

Angela sat up. "Bugs? What bugs?"

"There's no bugs. It's just what people say."

They waited for Angela to go to sleep. At ten minutes to eleven Debra whispered, "Let's go."

They got dressed and crawled out of the tent. "Wait," Debra said. "We need treats. Let's go back and get some more candy. I went in before supper and unlocked the window again."

"There's not going to be any candy bars left if we keep taking them."

"We'll just take four bars, that's all."

They let themselves in the commissary and helped themselves to the candy, then headed down to the lake. At the dock they sat down and waited. A few minutes later they heard someone coming. Michelle's heart was pounding with excitement.

The two boys, wearing jeans and leather jackets, came out on the dock and sat down. Michelle decided that in the dark they weren't too bad. After talking for a while, she asked the one she ended up with, who that night was calling himself

Tom, if she could wear his jacket. "What for? You cold?" he asked.

"No, I just like the way it smells."

He let her wear his jacket, then draped his arm around her. "I won it at a rodeo," he said. "Bull riding. It's kind of dangerous but, hey, who's afraid of a little danger, right?"

Michelle was sure he was lying but decided to play along anyway. "Cool," she said.

"I won mine at a rodeo too," the other boy, who called himself Luke, said, "—for bareback bronco riding."

"You guys aren't afraid of anything, are you," Debra said, really laying it on thick. "Can I wear your jacket too?"

"I guess so." Luke gave his jacket to her.

"What about you girls?" Tom asked.

"Shanna and I work as models in New York City," Debra said. "We're just out here for a vacation."

"New York, huh? Tom and I have rodeoed in New York before. Maybe sometime we could get together there after one of our rodeos." He paused a minute, then said, "So what do you two want to do now?"

"Let's go canoeing," Debra said.

"Sounds good."

They split up, Tom and Michelle in one canoe, Luke and Debra in another.

Tom and Michelle moved away and whispered together. Then they paddled as fast as they could toward the other canoe. Just before hitting it they sprayed Debra and Luke with their paddles. Debra screamed as the water hit her in the face and cried out, "You two are in deep, serious trouble!"

"You guys, I think maybe we're making too much noise," Michelle said.

It was too late. Up on the ridge someone carrying a flashlight was marching down to the lake. "Who's down there?"

There was only one thing to do—paddle to the other side of the lake. But Sister Drummond had played that game last night. She turned off her flashlight and crept along a trail beside the lake until she could hear voices. She stopped to listen. "Looks like we lost her," Luke said.

"We've got to go back to camp," Michelle said.

"Let's at least go swimming before you go."

"We didn't bring our swimsuits."

"You don't need swimsuits to go swimming."

That was enough for Sister Drummond. She shined her flashlight on them and stepped forward. "What on earth is going on here?"

"Nothing," Debra said.

"Nothing? You call sneaking off with a couple of boys nothing? You call using a canoe without supervision nothing? You call talking about swimming without anything on nothing? You boys, this is private property and you're trespassing. If you're not out of this camp in two minutes, I'm calling the sheriff."

The boys got back their leather jackets and then vanished into the night.

Sister Drummond's voice had carried back to camp. Suddenly out of nowhere other girls were coming down the trail. Sister Drummond heard them. "You girls go back to your tents this instant!"

The girls stopped but didn't go back. They stood on the trail and listened.

"This is the worst violation of girls camp rules I've ever seen," Sister Drummond scolded. "I'm calling your parents in the morning and having them come and take you both home."

Michelle was near tears. "Don't make us leave. We'll be good from now on. Please."

Sister Drummond thought about it. "Well, I can't promise anything, but I'll let you plead your case to the other leaders and we'll see what they think."

*　　　　　*　　　　　*

15

The next morning before flag ceremony a group of girls walked by the tent. "Hey, Michelle and Debra, there's a bunch of guys out here wanting to go swimming with you."

"I'm not going to flag ceremony," Michelle said to Debra.

Michelle's sixteen-year-old sister, Andrea, who was assigned to a section for older campers, stuck her head in. "Way to go, Michelle. Mom and Dad are going to kill you when they find out about this." She glared at Debra. "I know you're the one who talked Michelle into it."

"We did it together," Michelle said.

After flag ceremony and breakfast Sister Drummond came for the girls and escorted them to the area where the other leaders were waiting.

Debra presented her defense and concluded with, "Nothing happened."

"You disobeyed camp rules."

"We won't do it again," Michelle said. "Give us another chance. See, the thing is, Debra is all the time coming up with these crazy ideas but if I say no, then we don't do them. So let us stay and I'll make sure we don't do anything wrong again."

"Are you saying you'll take responsibility for Debra?"

"Yes. Like if she wants to do something wrong, I'll tell her we can't do that."

Sister Drummond couldn't decide what to do. "Is there anything else you two have done we don't know about?"

The girls looked at each other. And then Michelle, wanting to get everything out in the open, said, "Yes. We stole some candy bars from the commissary."

"We didn't actually steal 'em," Debra said. "We just sort of . . . borrowed 'em."

The girls were severely scolded and then told to wait in their tent while the leaders decided what to do. After a few minutes they were called back. Sister Drummond took charge. "We've decided to let you stay, provided you apologize to all

16

the girls in camp, pay back the price of the candy you stole, and obey all the camp rules from now on."

The other women left to oversee the day's activities, but Sister Drummond asked the girls to take a walk with her. They followed one of the trails a short distance into the woods and then stopped for Sister Drummond to sit down and catch her breath. "This is my last time to be at camp with you girls," she said. "I won't be back next year. My doctor says I can't do this anymore. I'm getting old." She paused. "It's been ten years. You want to know something? I don't like sleeping on the ground all that much."

"Then why do you come each year?" Debra asked.

"Because I love the young women of the Church. So when something like last night happens, I start to worry. This is not an easy world to grow up in. I want so much for you girls. I want you to see that living the gospel will bring you the greatest happiness in your life. Now's the time to decide, not when temptations come. I want you both to promise me you'll live worthy so you can go to the temple someday."

Michelle answered for them both. "We will."

Sister Drummond's eyes were moist with tears. She stood up and hugged them. On the way back, she asked, "How is Angela doing?"

"Okay."

"I'd like you two to try and include Angela more. In fact, I'll give you permission to use the canoe today if you take Angela along with you. I'll be there on the dock with the lifeguard, so you won't be breaking any of the rules."

They spent the afternoon paddling around with Angela. After a while that got boring, so they paddled over to the dock. Then, as they started to get out of the canoe, they rocked it until it tipped over. They had a great time.

That night in the tent, after Angela had fallen asleep, Michelle asked Debra if she was still awake.

"Yeah, sure."

"This morning when everyone was talking about us, I just wanted to crawl in a hole and never come out. I don't like feeling bad about something I've done. I don't ever want to feel this way again."

"Yeah, it wasn't much fun," Debra said.

"You remember asking me if I was going to wait until I got married before I . . . you know . . . Well, I've decided I'm going to wait. I don't want to feel guilty about things I did before I got married. I hope the boy I'll end up marrying is trying to live that way too."

"Wait, I can see him now . . . " Debra spoke in a solemn voice. "He's got this tablet of stone with these ten things written on them and he's coming down from this mountain . . . "

Michelle took her pillow and hit Debra over the head with it, which started a pillow fight between them, which woke Angela up, but this time she started laughing and joined in.

After it was over and everyone else was asleep, Michelle lay awake and thought about the boy who was growing up somewhere, the one she would marry some day.

2

Summer, 1983: Shane at Fifteen

That summer while Michelle was thirteen years old and growing up in Utah, Shane Robison was about to be a sophomore in high school and living in Billings, Montana.

At fifteen, Shane was beginning to look like the man he would someday become. He was nearly as tall as his father, with a ruddy complexion and hair the color of cornbread. He had always been a big boy. At times during grade school he would have been described as chubby, but now he was in a growth spurt and was becoming tall and lean. That summer he began to lift weights and work out every day. He wanted to be ready when football season began in August.

In May Shane had finally become an Eagle Scout. At that time it meant more to his parents than it did to him, but even so, he was glad to get it because it meant his parents finally let him drive. They had been holding that privilege hostage until he made Eagle. He didn't want his friends outside the Church to even know he was a Boy Scout, so when an article appeared in the newspaper about his becoming Eagle Scout, he was afraid they would make fun of him. But since few of them read the newspaper, his secret was safe.

Shane's sixteenth summer was important to him for another reason. It was the summer he faced the challenge of Gina Forsyth.

Of all the unlikely places to face a critical moral decision in his life, this was it — mowing lawns. He was trying to save up some money for his mission and also for some clothes in the fall.

The first few times he mowed the Forsyth lawn, he didn't even talk to Gina. She was a year older than he, but although he'd seen her before in school, they'd never spent any time together.

He tried to follow a schedule of mowing certain lawns on a particular day of the week. On Tuesday he usually did the Forsyths' first, then the Simonsons' down the street, and after lunch, the Wardells'.

The third time he came to mow the Forsyths' lawn, Gina was lying on a chaise lounge on the back patio, trying to get a tan. He mowed the front first and then the side. She was still outside so he started on the back lawn. When he stopped to empty the lawn clippings into the lawn bag, she came over. "You look hot and tired," she said. "Come in and I'll get you something to drink."

It was a hot day and he was thirsty, so he followed her inside.

She gave him a diet soda with ice, then asked if he was interested in computers. When he said yes, she invited him to see hers. She took him to her bedroom, had him sit at her desk, and turned on her PC. She showed him what she had learned, which wasn't much, then let him use it while she stood behind him and watched. He could feel her hair touching his cheek when she leaned over to say something. There was something about this that made him feel uneasy, but he couldn't put words to it. *I'm just using her computer,* he thought, *that's all.* And yet no matter how much he tried to argue himself out of it, he still felt that he shouldn't be there in her bedroom, especially with her wearing just a swimming suit. He stood up. "I'd better go finish up."

"Don't go. You've hardly rested at all."

"I'd better go. I have two more lawns to do today, and they said on the radio it might rain this afternoon."

"Come back and use my computer sometime when you're not in so much of a hurry."

"Sure, okay."

"My parents both work, in case you're wondering."

He hurried outside. He was glad to be away from her. He started up the lawn mower and began to finish up mowing. She didn't come out anymore that afternoon, but he knew she was watching him inside the house. He wondered why she'd told him her parents both worked.

After a while he took off his shirt. That wasn't unusual — he often did that when it was hot. But this time when he did it his face turned bright red because he knew she was watching and that he'd done it more for her than for anything else. By the time he finished the lawn, he felt as if he had a clamp around his chest that made breathing difficult. He also felt as if he'd done something very wrong, but when he tried to put words to it, it didn't sound wrong at all. He had taken his shirt off when he mowed his lawn. He had tried out someone else's computer. He had had a glass of diet soda with a girl. "So what's so bad about that?" he asked himself.

And yet no matter how he rationalized, he couldn't deny feeling guilty.

The next week he mowed the Forsyths' entire lawn with his shirt on even though it was the hottest day of the summer. Gina invited him in again. While he was sitting in the kitchen drinking a can of diet soda, she sat down next to him and passed him a plate of cookies. He grabbed a couple and took a big bite out of one. "Shane, I'm kind of interested in you . . . physically . . . if you know what I mean."

He stopped chewing his cookie and cleared his throat. He didn't know what to say. "I've got two other lawns to finish today and then I have to go home and clean the garage."

21

She smiled. "It doesn't have to be today. Some other time maybe."

"Are you talking about what I think you're talking about?"

"Yes. You're very nice to look at, Shane."

"I am?"

"Yes."

"Oh."

"Didn't you know that?"

"Not really. I didn't think girls looked at guys . . . that way."

"It's not just the way you look. I've been watching you. You're not like other guys around here. I know you wouldn't go around telling lies about me to everyone afterwards. You wouldn't tell anybody, would you?"

"No."

"I wouldn't say anything either. So nobody would know. It'd be our little secret."

He cleared his throat. "I should probably trim around the garden today. It's hard to mow there because the cucumber plants are coming out into the grass."

She smiled. "You need time to think about it, don't you." It was more a statement than a question.

"Yes."

"I understand. Look at it this way: how many offers like this are you going to get this summer?"

"Not many."

"That's right. The next time you come to mow, let me know if you're interested, okay?"

He went outside and trimmed the grass along the flower beds.

She came out before he left. "I just thought of something. When are you going to come back next week?"

"Tuesday."

"Thursday might be better."

"Why?"

"My parents are going on a trip on Thursday."

"Oh."

"So I'll be waiting for you on Thursday. Think about it, okay?"

She didn't need to ask him to think about it because for the next week that was all he could think about. At fifteen all the major goals in life seemed so far away . . . graduating from high school, a year of college, a mission, and then the time it would take to eventually find someone to marry. It seemed to him that the earliest he could get married was when he was twenty-two. That was seven years away. *I can wait seven long years or I can see Gina on Thursday,* he thought. *Seven years is a long time. I could be dead in seven years. Besides, like Gina says, guys don't turn down offers like this. At least I've never heard of any guy in school saying no. Oh sure, Joseph in the Bible said no to Potiphar's wife, but maybe she was ugly so it wasn't that tough to decide. I wish I knew what she looked like.*

Through the next week he couldn't decide what to do. One minute he'd tell himself he wouldn't go along with what Gina wanted; the next moment he changed his mind.

He didn't mow Gina's lawn on Tuesday as he usually did. He wasn't exactly sure why. *It's not because I've decided for sure,* he kept telling himself.

On Wednesday night his parents made him go to the wedding reception of Rebecca, a girl who used to baby-sit him when he was little. She'd been married in the temple to Andrew, a college student she met while working in West Yellowstone for the summer.

Shane noticed how happy they looked, but he was also aware from what his parents had told him that Andrew was twenty-five years old. Shane was almost sixteen. If it took him as long as it had taken Andrew to get married, he'd have to wait nine more years. Gina was there for him tomorrow, and all he had to do was show up at her house.

The next morning when he woke up he still hadn't decided

23

what to do. *This could be the day,* he thought. *Why wait? Why not just see what it's like?* He decided to take a shower to get clean, just in case. As he turned on the shower and stepped in, he knew it didn't make any sense to take a shower before he mowed a lawn because he would just get sweaty anyway, so why now, for the first time that summer, was he taking a shower before he went out to mow lawns?

He dried himself quickly. *Nine years or now,* he thought. *Nobody will need to know about it. I won't tell anyone and neither will Gina, so nobody will know except ourselves — and we won't ever talk about it afterwards.*

After he got dressed, without thinking, he put on some of his dad's after-shave, but he immediately washed it off because he hadn't made up his mind.

He looked at himself in the bathroom mirror. *If I go see Gina like she wants me to, what will I do if they ask me to prepare the sacrament table on Sunday? There's no rule that says I have to do that every Sunday. I can wear something other than a white shirt, and then they won't even ask me, or I can be late to church. But then what about the Sunday after that? What happens when I turn sixteen and the bishop interviews me for becoming a priest? Will I lie to him? I'll have to. I won't be able to ever tell anyone about this.*

There was a knock on the door. It was his mother. "Shane, breakfast is ready."

"I'm not hungry."

"You need to eat if you're going to be mowing lawns today."

He decided he'd better eat breakfast, but he worried that his mother or his sister, Megan, would smell the after-shave, so he washed his face again. When he entered the kitchen, his mother was making pancakes. Megan, who was twelve, and his little brother, Ben, were already eating. He looked at the clock. It was ten o'clock.

"Have you all had a chance to think about how happy Andrew and Rebecca were yesterday?" his mother said. "Your

24

father and I want you to be just as happy when you get married."
She brought over a stack of pancakes. "Ben, let's let Shane
have some before you have seconds, okay?" She sat down.
"What are some things you can do to prepare to be married
in the temple someday?"

"Make your bed every day," Ben said.

Shane thought that was the dumbest answer he'd ever
heard, but he didn't say anything because if he did he knew
his mother and Megan would side in with Ben.

"That's good, Ben. When you get married, your wife will
appreciate that you're willing to help out. Shane, what are you
doing to prepare for a temple marriage?"

Just then the telephone rang. His mother answered it. It
was the Relief Society president. Shane was glad it would be
a long call.

"Why do we have to have a sermon every time we eat
breakfast?" he complained to Megan.

"Maybe Mom thinks you need it," she teased.

"Very funny."

"Why'd you take a shower this morning?" Megan asked.
"Got a girl on the side we don't know about?"

"None of your business."

"Kind of touchy today, aren't you? Is that after-shave I
smell?"

"No, it's a new kind of shampoo."

"Yeah, right."

"I wish everyone would just leave me alone and let me
eat my stupid breakfast."

"Grumpy, grumpy, bumpy croc—i—dile," Ben said, recit-
ing from his favorite children's book.

"I have to go now."

"You still haven't told me why you took a shower this
morning," Megan said.

"Look who's talking," Shane shot back. "You take about
ten showers a day." He got up and left.

25

In the garage he checked the oil on the lawn mower, then filled the gas tank with gas. *I just want to know what it's like,* he thought. *Is that so bad? Everybody else has...Jenny and Bill, Jason and Nicole, Melissa and Michael, Nicole and Jimmy, Lisa and John, Jason and Erica.*

He realized that if he went all the way with Gina, it wouldn't stay a secret because if things like that could stay a secret, how come everybody in school knew about the others? He knew that if people started talking about him and Gina, eventually members of the Church his age would hear it and one of them would go talk to someone in the Church and before long the bishop would call him up and ask if he could talk to him. *And then I either have to lie or tell him the truth,* he thought. *Either way I'll end up feeling bad. And if Mom ever found out, she'd really be hurt. Dad would be disappointed and he'd probably never trust me after that.*

But just one time. Is one time going to hurt me that much? Just one time, just to find out what it's like. That's all. I wouldn't ever see Gina again. Just the one time. And then I'd live the way I'm supposed to for the rest of my life. What's so wrong with that?

He pushed the lawn mower down the street to Gina's home. He still wasn't sure what he was going to do, except he realized that if he went in her house, he pretty much knew what would happen.

He walked around her lawn one time because last week he'd mowed over a kid's baseball glove, so now he checked every time before he mowed.

Gina came out. "I knew you'd be coming today," she said.

He felt guilty just talking to her. He wondered if any neighbors were watching them.

"When do you want ... uh ... to have some lemonade, now or later?" she asked.

For some reason when he looked at her it reminded him of last winter when the flu was going around. People got the flu from others and then gave it to their friends. *That's what this is like,* he thought. *It's like a disease that's going around at school. It's like Gina is part of an epidemic and she's picked me to be the next one to get the disease.*

She put her hand on his shoulder while he worked on the mower. It reminded him of their cat Sylvester. Most of the time Sylvester didn't want to have anything to do with the family, but when it was time to be fed, he always came up and rubbed himself across the leg of whoever was in the kitchen. It was like he was saying, "You are my most favorite one in this family," but then after you set out his cat food and he'd eaten it, he didn't care about you anymore and went to the door to be let out.

Shane knew he would be the same way. He knew he would never call Gina again after that first time. He might even get someone else to mow the Forsyths' lawn. All he really wanted was to know what it was like, and he had no interest in her, not really. And the guys in school who'd done it with someone, most of them never went back to the girl. After today he'd never want to see her again. He didn't want romance or even friendship; all he wanted was to find out what it was like.

He knew what it was like to go through the process of repentance. He had already gone through that once when he had an interview with the bishop and the bishop asked him if he'd ever cheated on an exam. He had once. He remembered how bad he felt having to admit he'd done wrong, and he didn't want to ever go through that again. The bishop was calm and everything, but for Shane to have to tell him something he'd done in secret was one of the most difficult things he'd ever had to do.

This'll never stay a secret, he thought. *Even if neither one of us talks to anyone about it, eventually I'll feel so bad I'll end up going to the bishop, because if I don't, I'll never feel good about myself again. It's not fair. I want to know what it's like but I can't do it for a long time. It's just not fair.*

27

She was walking toward the house and he, almost against his will, was following her.

"Where are your parents?" he asked.

"They're away on business," she said.

"No kidding? What business is your dad in?"

She turned to face him. "Do you really care?"

"No."

"I didn't think so. Let's go inside, okay?"

She opened the door and went in. He stood there frozen in place on the steps. She turned around. "Are you coming in or not?"

He felt his heart racing. It was difficult to think. His mind seemed far away, almost detached from the rest of his body. Suddenly he was certain that Potiphar's wife in the Bible was probably even more sexy than Gina. Maybe Joseph had even considered staying with her.

Gina, seeing his reluctance, came back outside. "Don't you like me?"

Now he knew why Joseph ran from Potiphar's wife. This was not a time for listing reasons for chastity. This was a time to run away, because if he didn't run away, he would stay—and if he stayed, he would be sorry.

"I forgot my clippers. I have to go back and get them." He knew it didn't make sense, but it didn't matter. He didn't wait for an answer. He left the mower on the front lawn and ran home.

When he got home he found out that his mother and Ben had gone to buy groceries. Megan was practicing piano.

"I need you to help me," he said.

"Doing what?"

"Clipping along a fence at somebody's house while I mow the lawn."

"I'm busy."

"I'll pay you."

"You've never asked me to help you before. Why are you asking me now?"

"There's this girl in one of the places where I mow."

"Yeah, so?"

"I don't want to be alone with her."

"A girl is coming on to you? Is she blind or what?"

"Megan, just come with me, okay?"

"Okay, let me change first."

He called out just before she went in her room, "Promise you won't say anything to Mom or Dad about this, okay?"

"Yeah, sure."

A few minutes later they started for Gina's house.

"What's she like?"

"She's good-looking."

"Is that all you know about her?"

"Yes."

They reached Gina's house. They could hear music coming from inside and the front door was open.

"Is she waiting for you?" Megan asked as he primed the lawn mower.

"Yeah."

"You're not all that sure you want to stay out here, right?"

"Not completely."

"So I'm here to make sure you don't get into trouble, is that it?"

"Yes, that's it."

"Do you want me to do anything while I'm here besides keep an eye on you?"

"You might as well trim along the edges with the Weed Whacker. I'll pay you."

"How much?"

"A dollar."

"A dollar? Is that all?"

"Two dollars then."

"Three."

"Two and a half."

"All right."

Shane reached down and started up the mower. It made a deafening sound. He looked at the house and saw a curtain in her bedroom move aside and then drop back to its original position.

By the time he was ready to start on the back, Mr. and Mrs. Forsyth pulled into the driveway. They were supposed to be out of town. The car they were driving wasn't their car. Shane turned off the mower, and Mr. Forsyth said hello to him.

"New car?" Shane asked.

"It's a rental. The transmission on our car went out on us on the interstate. We were going on a trip, but that's out for us now."

"Is Gina inside?" her mother asked.

"Yes, I think so. Have you met my sister, Megan? She's helping me today."

"Hello, Megan. Excuse me, I need to talk to Gina."

A minute later from her bedroom window, he heard Gina say, "Mom, what are you doing here?"

"What is going on here?" Her mother came over and closed the window, and he didn't hear what happened after that.

Megan came up to him. "Are you thinking what I'm thinking?"

"Yeah."

"Good choice, Shane."

From then on, Megan came with him when he mowed Gina's lawn. Even though he saw Gina in school after that, he never talked to her again.

3

October 1984: Michelle and Debra at Fourteen

More than a year had passed. Even though Michelle and Debra lived next to each other and saw each other every day, they spent much of their lives on the phone. So much, in fact, that their fathers both got their daughters a teen line so others would have a chance to use the phone.

There was lots for the two girls to talk about. They were now ninth graders and in the big league as far as meeting and talking to boys. They were both tall for their age, and because they liked attention, they refused to wear "little girl" clothes that would give their age away.

Because of the pledge they'd made to each other at girls camp, Michelle still felt responsible to make sure Debra stayed out of trouble.

Phone conversation October 10:

"Guess who just called me?" Debra asked. "Josh Carter."

"Josh Carter, the senior? What'd he want?"

"He wanted to know if I'd go out with him on Friday."

"Did you tell him you can't date until you're sixteen?"

"Why would I tell him that?"

"You're not going to go out with him, are you?"

"It's just to the game and then the dance afterwards."

31

"I don't think you should do that."

"Why not?"

"You know what the Church says about not dating until you turn sixteen."

"I'm not going to sit around and do nothing until I turn sixteen."

"You think your mom and dad will let you?" Michelle asked.

"I won't tell 'em. I'll go with you to the game and then meet Josh there. Don't say anything, okay?"

Phone conversation October 13:

"We had soooo much fun last night," Debra said. "We went to the house of a friend of Josh's and watched some movies. Most everybody else there was a senior, but they treated me just like I was one of them." She paused. "What did you do after the game?"

Michelle hated to admit it. "I did homework."

"I told Josh about you and he says he has a friend, like if the four of us ever wanted to go out."

"My parents won't let me until I'm sixteen."

"Why not? Don't they want you to have any fun?"

"You can have fun without dating. Like next Friday at church we're having a game night."

"Boys our age are so dumb . . . especially compared to somebody like Josh."

"Was anybody drinking last night?"

"Some were, but so what? It's no big deal. Don't worry about it. Nothing happened."

The next weekend at the church party for fourteen- and fifteen-year-olds, Michelle got Debra to go instead of going out with Josh. After being at the party for half an hour, Debra told Michelle that Josh was going to pick her up in the parking lot.

32

"Stay here. Don't go with him."

"No. It's so boring here, I can't stand it."

"Let me go with you then."

"The two of us and Josh?"

"Why not?"

"That wouldn't work."

"Why are you going out with Josh again?"

"Because it's more fun than this."

"When will you be back?"

"At eleven. I'll go home with you so my mom and dad won't suspect anything."

Michelle stood at the door while Debra waited. She tried to talk Debra out of going, but nothing she said seemed to make any difference.

Josh's car pulled up. Debra looked back. "I'll see you at eleven, okay? Look, don't worry, nothing's going to happen. I'll be back at eleven and then we'll call my mom and ask her to come and give us a ride home."

The party ended at eleven. Michelle's sister Andrea asked if she wanted a ride home, but Michelle said she was going to help clean up. One by one everybody left until finally it was just Michelle and the Young Women's president, who asked, "Do you need a ride home?"

"No, that's okay. My mom's going to pick me up. She'll be here any minute. You can go home now. I'll be all right."

"I'm not supposed to leave until everyone else is gone."

"I called my mom. She's on her way. It'll just be a minute. You go."

"Well, okay, if your mom is on her way."

Michelle stood in the semidarkness just inside the door to the church, waiting for Debra. At eleven thirty Josh's car pulled up. Michelle opened the door of the church so Debra would know she was there. Debra said goodbye to Josh, then ran up the stairs.

"Where have you been?"

"We lost track of the time. Sorry."

Michelle glared at her.

"Nothing happened," Debra said.

"You keep saying nothing happened but something is happening."

"What?"

"Things are only exciting to you now if they're against what the Church teaches."

They were standing just inside the door. The dull red glow from the exit sign was their only source of light.

"I was worried when you didn't come," Michelle said.

"You didn't need to worry so much. Nothing happened. We'd better call my mom now, okay? We need a reason why we're so late. Got any ideas?"

"We helped clean up."

"Good. We'll use that."

After the phone call, they went back by the door to wait.

"What did you do after I left?" Debra asked.

"We played Pictionary, the boys against the girls."

"Oh."

"You think that sounds dumb, don't you."

"I didn't say that."

"No, but you were thinking it."

"Josh's car can go one hundred miles an hour. He showed me on our way back."

"On the way back from where?"

"I don't know where we were, but it's up in the mountains. It's a place he likes to go at night."

Debra's mother pulled up. They made sure the church door locked behind them, then ran out and got in the car. "Sorry we're so late, but we had to help clean up," Debra said.

Michelle played second-chair cello in the high school orchestra. First-chair was Elliott Sandberg. Elliott's father taught

34

political science at the University of Utah. The family had moved to Salt Lake City a year ago from Trenton, New Jersey.

To almost anybody Elliott would have seemed a little strange, but to the students at his school, it was like he came from another planet. He had a thick eastern accent, but more than that, he lived in the world of ideas. He used language like a carpenter uses wood. Both his parents had doctoral degrees, and both of them worked full-time as professionals. His mother, an M.D., was an internist at the University of Utah Medical Center.

Once Michelle ate supper over at Elliott's house. She felt as if she should have studied before she went there, but they were very good to her and asked her opinions and didn't attack them as they might have if she'd been a member of the family.

His parents were members of the Church from birth but now were slightly amused by it. Elliott, possibly as a form of rebellion, was totally devoted to it.

Michelle saw Elliott in orchestra every day. Because they were in the same ward and close to the same age, they were thrown together a lot. Elliott didn't have a lot of friends. He didn't fit in with the other high school students. He didn't like sports or fishing or hunting or cars.

That year Michelle became Elliott's best friend. She teased him about challenging him and taking over the first-chair position, but she never did because she knew he was so much better than she was.

That fall, for the first time in his life, Elliott bore his testimony during a testimony meeting. "My dad asked me why I was reading the Book of Mormon, and I told him it was because I thought it was important to know what was in it. He told me not to waste valuable study time. I asked him if he'd ever read it, and he said no, not all of it. But now I have." And then he paused. "I've read it." He stopped again. Tears were filling his eyes. "I prayed about it."

People who had been nodding off looked up. With his

voice cracking, Elliott said, "It's really true." And then he sat down.

After the meeting was over, Michelle went up and hugged Elliott.

"What's that for?" he asked.

"For being you."

"Who else could I be?"

"Don't spoil it, okay?"

"Okay." As she started to leave, he asked, "Does this mean you're going with me?"

"It means I think maybe you're human after all, Elliott, that's all it means." She looked back at him. He was smiling. She wished he would smile more often. Maybe sometime she'd mention it to him. The only problem was, with Elliott there were so many things to mention.

Friday nights were the worst for Michelle, knowing that Debra was out with Josh, while she sat at home, practicing cello, doing homework, watching movies on the VCR, listening to her mom asking her to clean her room.

The nights Debra was out with Josh were the worst for her because she knew the next day Debra would call her and tell her all about it. She'd sit and listen, and when it was over she'd be more worried about Debra but also she'd end up feeling that life was passing her by, that everybody else was having fun except her.

One particular Friday night was worse than usual. She'd had tests all week and an essay for English class that had kept her up late the night before. Debra had gone to a movie with Josh.

"Michelle, when do you think you'll be able to get to your room?"

It was the last straw. "I'll get to it sometime, Mom. Do you have to keep bringing it up every ten minutes?"

"Is anything wrong?"

"I'm just tired of you hassling me all the time, that's all."

"Sorry. Let me help you. Is now a good time?"

It had been a hard week and she hadn't spent any time on cleaning up. On the floor was a pile of clothes she'd worn on Monday, another pile from Tuesday, and so forth through the week.

"I'm sorry I'm so messy," Michelle said.

"You're busy."

"Why can't I date until I'm sixteen?"

Her mother looked at her. "You know why."

"It's not fair. Other girls go out before they're sixteen. Why can't I? I'm tired of staying home all the time. You keep telling me I'm mature for my age. Well, if that's true, then why can't I start going out with guys?"

"Has anyone asked you?"

"No, nobody's asked me, but they probably would have if you hadn't told the whole world I'm not going to start dating until I turn sixteen."

"I don't know all the reasons why the Church has asked this of you, but I do know that a sixteen-year-old girl has a much more solid sense of her own worth than a fourteen-year-old."

Answers like that really made Michelle mad. "What has that got to do with anything?"

"If you don't know who you are, then you can be talked into things that aren't good for you."

"If someone asked me to go out, would you let me?"

"No."

"Why not?"

"Because this is not a time in your life for dating."

"What is it a time for then? Staying in my room? Being alone all the time?"

"This is a time of preparation."

"I'm tired of preparing. I'm tired of school. I'm tired of

Elliott talking to me about all the stupid books he's read. I'm tired of practicing every day. I'm tired of doing homework. I'm tired of trying to be this perfect little person all the time. I'm tired of listening to girls my age tell about the guys they're going with. I'm tired of everything."

"What do you want to change in your life?"

"I want to have someone I can talk to about anything without worrying I've opened myself up too much. I want somebody who understands me."

"What you're talking about is what happens in a good marriage."

"I don't want to get married. I just think there ought to be more out of life than this. I never have any fun anymore."

"Never?"

"Not like some girls."

"Would you like to have some people over next Friday night?"

"No, Mom, I don't want that."

"Why not?"

"Because I've had parties before so I know what would happen. You'd sit down with me and we'd make up this list of things you have to do to have a party, like inviting people, and figuring out what we were going to eat, and what things we were going to do at the party, and then I'd work on it all week, and then we'd have the party, and everybody'd have a nice time, and they'd all go home, so I'd have gone to all that work and it still wouldn't be what I wanted it to be."

"What would you want a party to be?"

"Fun without any work."

"The good things in life always require preparation. Parties do, but love and intimacy do too. There are no shortcuts to happiness."

"Is that why I can't date?"

"Yes."

"It's not fair."

"Do you have any idea how wonderful you are? I want you to have all the best that life has to offer. It will come to you if you're patient and prepare for it. Just hang in there, okay?"

"Okay."

"I've got an idea. Let's all go out for ice cream, like we used to."

"You're on a diet."

"I'm always on a diet. Come on, let's treat ourselves tonight. We deserve something for doing all this work on a Friday night, don't we?"

Andrea, the only one of her three older sisters who was still living at home, was out with friends that night; but her father and her younger brother, Billy, came along too. Michelle didn't really care about the ice cream, but she went anyway because it was something her parents thought she would enjoy, and in spite of herself, she did enjoy it.

That night as she got ready for bed, she went to the window and looked out. She thought about the boy she'd marry some-day. *I'm saving myself for you,* she thought. *I hope you're doing the same for me. I wish I could talk to you. Where are you and what are you doing right now? Do you ever get lonely?* She paused and wished she were magic and could see him but she knew she couldn't, so instead she daydreamed about him, wherever he was.

4

October 1984: Shane at Sixteen

During his junior year of high school, if Shane had to admit who was the most important person in his life, it wouldn't have been a girl at all. It was Matt Stone.

They both went out for football that fall. Matt wanted to be a quarterback and throw the ball. Shane wanted to catch passes and run for touchdowns. Unfortunately the coach wanted them both to sit on the bench.

For the first three games they didn't play at all. But it wasn't that bad sitting on the bench. For one thing, you never got your uniform dirty and you never got hurt. Besides that, girls didn't seem to know who had played anyway. Shane and Matt liked to go to the school dance after each game and walk up to a girl and say, "Hey, did you see the great play I made tonight? You know, the one where I ran in for a touchdown."

"Oh yeah, that was really good."

Once the two of them got together at one of the after-school dances and made a bet to see who could tell the biggest lie to a girl and have her believe him. Matt won by saying he had scored three touchdowns in a game that ended with the score 7 to 0.

On the fourth game of the season, their team couldn't seem to do anything right. They were already behind 21 to 0 when

40

the regular quarterback got hurt, just seconds before the half ended. "Stone, you'll be playing second half," the coach said in the locker room during halftime.

"Me?" Matt asked.

"Try not to embarrass us any more than we already are, okay?"

"I need Shane in there with me."

"What for?"

"We've practiced together. We can read each other's mind."

"All right, we'll try it and see how it goes."

Just before the second half was to begin, Matt asked Shane if he was nervous.

"A little."

"Don't be. The coach has already written the game off. Let's just have a fun time—okay?—and not worry about anything else. What's the longest pass that's ever been thrown here?"

"I don't know. Why?"

"Let's beat the record."

In the huddle the first time they got the ball, Matt turned to Shane. "Run a post pattern as deep as you can. I'll hit you between the numbers."

"The coach doesn't like us to pass much," one of the seniors muttered.

"Hey, I'm the quarterback now. We'll do it my way."

When the ball was snapped, Shane hit the man opposite him, rolled to the side, and ran as fast as he could. Because the seniors didn't like some sophomore hotshot telling them what to do, the line didn't give Matt much pass protection, so he had to scramble around some before he stopped, located Shane, and threw deep.

The ball was overthrown, but Shane ran as fast as he could, reached out, and just touched it, flipping it up in the air. When it came down again, he grabbed it and ran in for the touchdown.

The die-hard fans who were still watching the game went

41

crazy. People stood up while the band played the school song. Shane ran back to Matt and threw his arms around him.

"Easy, man. You're worse than the other team," Matt joked.

"We did it!"

"Yeah, right. Quick, take off your helmet."

"What for?"

"So the girls can see it was us."

The next time they got the ball, Matt called the same play.

"You can't do the same play again," the same senior objected.

"Where does it say that?"

"They'll be expecting it this time."

"I don't care. Shane can catch anything. Shane, run deep and then at the last minute run to the far left. I'll hit you there."

Shane lined up across from the man he'd beat out for the first touchdown.

"You got lucky the last time."

"You're right."

Shane got nailed, fell down, and started running, but wasn't able to get to the ball.

"Same play," Matt said in the huddle.

"This is ridiculous. How about a running play?"

"No, I'll pass again."

Again, an incomplete pass. The coach sent in a play. It was a running play.

"We'll pass again," Matt said.

"Why?"

"Because everybody knows the coach sent in a play. And no coach in the world would call in another passing play. That would be stupid, so that's why we're going to do it."

"The coach is going to take you out of the game."

"If he does, he does. Passing play."

Shane lined up.

"Running play, right?"

"Right."

Shane blocked halfheartedly and then ran for the end zone.

This time the ball was underthrown. He had to run up five yards, catch it, and then reverse direction. Just after catching the ball, he looked down and saw eleven guys, like large freight trains, heading his way. He ran for his life and managed to cross the end zone before they caught up to him.

Even though they'd got another touchdown, the coach was furious with Matt for not running the play he'd called in. He railed on Matt unmercifully while the other team ran the ball play after play, grinding their way in three- and four-yard runs every play until they got another touchdown, making the score 28 to 14. "From now on, do what I say when I send in a play," the coach yelled.

"Coach, everybody is watching you chew me out, right?"

"So?"

"So they all expect me to run the next time it's third down and I've thrown on the first two downs."

"So?"

"Could we maybe take advantage of that?"

The coach thought about it and said, "Try it once. We'll see if it works."

It worked one more time; the final score was 28 to 21. Even though they'd lost, the fans liked Matt's style. When a game seemed hopeless they would start chanting, "We want Stone . . . We want Stone."

The coach put Matt and Shane in a game either when they were so far behind that it was hopeless, or when they were so far ahead that the other team could never catch up with them. He never trusted the two completely. Privately, to his wife, he called them "loose cannons."

But by the time the season ended, they were an accepted part of the team. They both bought letter jackets, which they wore every chance they got, not only to impress the girls but also because they'd been through so much as a team. They had learned to depend on each other when times got tough.

Matt wasn't a Mormon, but he did attend his church with his parents. Despite their differences, Matt and Shane had many attitudes in common. They both thought that drinking was dumb. They both had some disappointing experiences with girls and liked to tease each other about them. They both did imitations of several guys they saw in school: the cowboy types who hung around by their pickups before classes began, the ones who liked to talk in great detail about what they'd done to their car's engine, and finally those who drank every weekend and then bragged about how gross they'd become.

Matt's locker was so far away from where he had most of his classes that they decided to share a locker. In order to have enough room, they designed and then built shelves for their locker. The trick was to show it off to other students but not let the school staff know about what they'd done.

They used little sticky pads to write notes to each other during the day. It was their form of "phone calls."

Notes between Shane and Matt posted in their locker:

1. Matt, these sticky sheets of paper are for you and me to leave messages on. Good idea, huh? Don't waste them, ok?

2. How would you like to own a beautiful pair of Rayban Wayfarer Sunglasses?

3. Shane, who put the dent in your Carmex?

4. I was here at 7:35. Where were you? Been asked out yet?

5. A teacher just walked by and eyed our locker.

6. How about these tests, Poncho? Lotsa fun.

7. Matt, you will open this locker 630 times this year.

8. Shane, let's paint our locker inside. It has the potential of being totally yellow inside.

9. Who said we should paint our stupid locker anyway? It smells.

10. It will go away.

11. It still smells.

12. Hey, Shane, it's Friday. Party till you puke, right? Just like all the others around here.

13. I saw you in the library with Jennifer. What are you trying to do, study yourself into a relationship?

14. Just friends. Have you seen my Ray Bans?

15. Matt, she's not going to collect or grade the chemistry assignment today. Let's go out, okay?

16. Pencil shortage, Shane.

17. It's a race day. See who can collect the most pencils by fifth period. Let's make the pencil shortage a fun part of our lives!

18. I took some of your gum.

19. May your toes rot out and your ions be all messed up.

For a while they had enough bad luck with girls that they decided to make a game out of it. They tried to find out which girls were grounded and then call them up and ask them out. It was the perfect plan. The girls felt bad because they were grounded, and the boys didn't actually have to go out with them.

Shane made the mistake of telling someone about only asking out girls who were grounded. Before long two girls decided to teach Matt and Shane a lesson. They told everybody they were grounded.

The boys took the bait. "Say, Allison, Matt and I are planning on going to the Jade Palace restaurant, having their famous lobster-and-steak dinner, and then going to see the musical *Camelot*. Would you be able to go with me?"

"Gosh, isn't that expensive?"

"Oh sure, but you know us, nothing's too good for the girls we go out with."

"When are you going?"

"Friday night."

"I'd love to. Thanks for asking me."

45

"Uh, it's *this* Friday."

"I can go this Friday."

"You're not grounded or anything?"

"No, why do you ask?"

"No reason. You'll be able to go then?"

"Yes, I'll look forward to it. I've always wanted to eat at the Jade Palace restaurant but nobody I've ever gone out with has been able to afford it."

Shane panicked. "Let's see. Matt is planning on asking Julia. If she can't go, then maybe we'll have to do it some other time."

"I'm pretty sure she can go."

"Maybe she's grounded."

"No, I don't think so. I'll see you on Friday, Shane. Thanks a lot."

The next day the two boys met at their locker.

"You and your stupid ideas," Shane said.

"My stupid idea? It was *your* stupid idea."

They took the girls out for supper, but then they lied and said the play was sold out.

"Are you sure?" Allison said. "Why don't we call the box office and see? Maybe somebody had some tickets reserved but can't make it."

"No, we don't want to call up," Matt said quickly, seeing another large dent in his funds coming up.

"You sound like you really don't want to take us to the play," Julia said.

"Of course we do."

"Then let's call up and see if they have any tickets."

They ended up taking the girls to the play, but since they didn't have enough money for four tickets, Matt and Shane offered to wait in the car until the play was over. The girls, out for revenge, accepted their kind offer.

"You and your dumb ideas," Matt complained as they sat in the car.

"That's it. I'm through with girls. Girls, shmirls, that's my motto from now on."

One of the reasons Shane liked to go to early-morning seminary was because Jennifer Morrison would be there. She was fun to talk to and good looking. Her one drawback was that she wasn't overly impressed with Shane's football glory.

"How come you never take that thing off in seminary?" she asked, referring to his letterman jacket.

"It's cold in here."

"I'm not cold."

"Girls have more fat than guys."

"Thanks a lot, Shane."

"It's a fact. I read it somewhere."

"Don't change the subject. We were talking about your letter jacket. Do you need to wear it all the time to prove how much of a man you are?"

"I don't have to prove anything."

"Then what's your problem?"

"There's no problem."

"Then why do you wear that coat all the time?"

"You wouldn't understand."

"Try me."

"The guys on the team, we have to depend on each other ... I mean, if any one of us doesn't do our job, then we all pay for it."

"It's male bonding then, right?"

Shane didn't know what that meant, but it didn't sound normal. "Absolutely not."

"You football players are so funny to watch."

"Why's that?"

"You walk around like you own the school, like everybody else is just dirt under your feet. You want to know something?

Nobody cares that much about your football season. You won a few games and you lost a few games. Big deal."

"Wait until next year. We're going to take the state championship."

"It won't make any difference to me if you do. Look, I haven't wanted to tell you, but the truth is, I can hardly stand to be around you anymore."

"Why?"

"The way you treat other people. It's like you're looking down on the rest of the world and only your opinions are important. That thing you and Matt did about asking girls out who were grounded was really a stupid thing to do."

Shane cleared his throat. Nobody had ever talked to him that way.

"Most of the girls in school think you and Matt are scum. I just thought you'd like to know."

"I don't care."

"I guess maybe they're right then." She got up and found another place to sit for seminary.

He stared at her through class but she wouldn't look at him. *So what?* he thought. *I don't need her. Girls, shmirls.*

In March, as the day of the Junior Prom approached, Shane's mother suggested that if he was going to ask someone, he should do it in plenty of time so the girl could get ready for the dance. He decided to talk to Matt about it.

"I say we don't go," Matt said.

"I say if we do go, we wait until the last minute before we ask 'em."

That night after supper, Shane's mother suggested he take Jennifer.

"No."

"Why not?"

"We're not that close."

"You're in seminary together all the time."

"She doesn't like me anymore."

"There's not that many Mormon boys in school she could go with. Besides, you two really do like each other, don't you?"

"We see each other every morning. I've seen her without makeup and she's noticed things about me she can't stand."

"But you're friends. I think you should ask her to the prom."

"Why go at all? It's not that big of a deal."

"It is to a girl."

"Then let her ask me."

"Shane, quit being so bullheaded and ask her."

"No, Matt and I have an agreement."

"What's your agreement?"

"Girls, shmirls."

"Ask Jennifer to the prom. It means so much to a girl to be asked to a nice dance like that."

"I'm not asking Jennifer."

"Why not?"

"Because that's what everyone expects."

Shane was stubborn and didn't ask Jennifer to the prom. Instead he asked Samantha, a friend of the girl Matt had asked. Their date began at five in the afternoon with hors d'oeuvres at Samantha's house, followed by supper at a restaurant, and then the dance.

At eleven o'clock, while their dates were in the restroom, Matt complained to Shane. "Why is it we're spending so much money on this thing and I'm so bored? Whatever I say, all Christina does is smile. I even insulted her one time and she smiled."

"Let's go outside for a minute. I need some air. Samantha's perfume makes my eyes water."

They went outside. "Do you realize how much this is costing us?" Matt asked.

"It was a mistake to have asked anyone."

Matt looked at his watch. "The worst thing is, we still got three hours left."

"You got that football in your trunk?" Shane asked.

"Yeah, sure. Why?"

"Why don't we throw it around in the parking lot for a while?"

They went out to the parking lot and threw the ball back and forth.

"You suppose we should go in and ask the girls if they want to do this with us?" Shane asked.

"No. They'll just make us feel guilty we abandoned them."

"We didn't abandon them. Besides, they go to the girls' room together, we do this together. I say it's fair."

Jennifer came outside. "What are you two doing?"

"What does it look like we're doing?"

"Shane, can I talk to you alone for a minute?"

They walked over to an area where they could be alone. "Why are you being such a jerk?" she asked.

"I guess it just comes natural. Why do you care anyway?"

"Sometimes I'm embarrassed to tell people you're a member of the Church. You walk around like you're God's gift to girls, but you're not. You don't know the first thing about girls. You think they care about you catching some dumb ball during a football game. That's not important to most girls. It's not important to me, I'll tell you that. Why don't you grow up?"

"Just because I'm not the way you think a guy should be doesn't mean I'm not grown up."

"Listen to me. You've got to go back in there and dance with Samantha. You can't stay outside with Matt."

"I should've asked you to the prom. At least we argue. That's more than I've got going with Samantha."

"I'm not sure I'd have gone with you if you'd asked me."

"Why not?"

"You know why. Look, go back to the dance. It's your job to make sure Samantha has a good time tonight."

"Since when is it my job?"

"After you asked her out, she called me up. She wanted to know what you were like."

"So you told her I was a jerk, right?"

"No." She paused. "I told her you were a nice guy."

"You did?"

"Yes."

"What else?"

"I told her how important the Church was to you. Be good to her, Shane. She's my friend. She might even join the Church someday."

He sighed. "All right."

He went back to Matt. "Let's go back in and dance."

"Is that what Jennifer told you to do?"

"Yes."

"You like her, don't you," Matt observed.

"Maybe. C'mon, we have to go back in."

"Why? It's more fun out here."

"We have to make sure our dates have a nice time tonight."

"Who says?"

"Jennifer."

"You two have a weird thing going between you, do you know that?"

"You wouldn't understand."

"You're right there."

They went inside. Shane did his best to give Samantha a good memory of her night at the Junior Prom.

On his way home after the dance he felt as if nobody really understood him. He wondered if he'd ever be able to find someone who would. So far it didn't look too promising. Except for Jennifer.

He smiled. *Maybe I'll marry her someday,* he thought.

5

September 1985: Michelle and Debra at Fifteen

Debra glanced at Dave as he drove her home. She wanted him to tell her he still liked her but she knew he wouldn't because he never talked much after they had sex in the back seat of his car.

She'd first started going out with him last May. After being pressured by him for weeks to have sex, she agreed to it in July. She thought it would bring them closer, but it hadn't. If anything, Dave seemed afraid of being trapped into having to make a commitment. There was no romance, no magic, no funny times between them anymore. She wanted him to show her that he cared about her, but all she seemed to get from him was silence. He didn't like to talk about his feelings. He didn't even hold her hand when they walked down the halls at school anymore. She wanted him to say he was more committed to her now than before, but he didn't. She wanted him to tell her that if she got pregnant he'd stand by her and marry her if that's what she wanted, but he didn't.

Earlier that night as he had driven her to the secluded place where they made love, he didn't even hold her hand. Except for the radio, they sat in silence. Once they arrived he kissed her a couple of times, then said, "Get in the back seat."

"Dave, we need to talk."

"What about?"

"Do you even like me anymore?"

"Yeah, sure, you know I do." He seemed mad at her for bringing it up. He got out of the car, opened the back door, and then stared at her. "Well, you coming back here or not?"

"Not tonight. All we ever do anymore is come out here."

"Don't give me that. You like it as much as I do—admit it. Are you coming back here or not?"

"No."

He slammed his fist into the side of the car. "What did we come out here for anyway?" He swore and stormed away.

After a few minutes he got back in the car and acted as if nothing had happened. He started kissing her. She knew he was trying to get her to want to go in the back seat with him.

She didn't mean to, but eventually she gave in. When it was over, he didn't say anything. And as they drove back to town, she knew he didn't really care about her, not really, not the way she wanted him to. None of this was the way she thought it would be.

When he let her out in front of her house, she had to say something. "I don't want to do this anymore, Dave."

"Fine then, it's no big deal, either way."

"I didn't say I wanted to break up with you. I just think we should talk about things."

"You want to know something? I'm really getting tired of your whining all the time. Get out now, okay?"

"I don't want to break up with you."

"What do you want then?"

"I want you to show me you care about me."

"You want to know what I want? I want out. This is getting too complicated. We've had our fun—now let's give it up, okay?"

"Why won't you just listen to what I have to say?"

"About what?"

"About us."

"There's nothing to say. Look, why don't you just get out of the car so I can leave."

"None of this meant anything to you, did it?"

"What'd you expect? True love?"

She held back her tears because she didn't want him to see her cry. Inside the house her mother asked her how the dance at church was. She said it was fine and then went to her room. She forced herself not to cry while she got ready for bed, and then she turned off all the lights and let the tears come silently. She felt abandoned. She had never felt more alone in her life. *I should have listened to what people in school said about Dave,* she thought. *They tried to tell me about him but I wouldn't listen. Well, they were right.*

She looked across the yard to Michelle's bedroom. All the lights in the house were out. *She's asleep,* she thought, *just like a good girl should be . . . just like I used to be. I wish I could go back to the way it was before I met Dave.*

It was late and Michelle was asleep, but she had a teen-line phone in her room. Maybe she'd answer it before her parents woke up and wondered what was going on. Debra punched in the number and waited. *C'mon, Michelle, wake up, wake up,* she said to herself.

Michelle answered on the third ring. "Hello," she said sleepily.

"I have to talk to you. I feel awful."

"What's wrong?"

"Dave broke up with me. He never really cared about me anyway." She paused. "I gave him everything he wanted."

"You did?"

"Yes."

"I thought you said you weren't going to do that."

"He talked me into it."

"Are you pregnant?"

"I don't think so, but I'm not sure."

"What will you do if you get pregnant?"

"I don't know. I won't marry Dave, that's for sure. I don't even like him anymore." She paused. "You remember that night in the canoe when we promised each other we'd help each other out? Well, I need your help now."

"What do you want me to do?"

"Make it be like it was before Dave."

March 1986: Michelle and Debra

Once a month Bishop Kenner had a fireside in his home. It was his fireside and he planned the program. On this night he got up and said he'd like each of the youths to bear their testimonies.

They had expected something more fun. At first there was silence and then, one by one, they each got up and talked.

The rest of the group sat and listened and thought.

Debra knew she would be expected to say something, but she didn't know what to say. It had been six months since she'd quit seeing Dave, but she still felt like she didn't belong at church. It wasn't that people treated her badly; it was more the feeling that the Church wasn't for people like her who had made really serious mistakes.

She was trying to live the right way. She went to church and seminary and Young Women's activities. She didn't hang out in places where she might see any of Dave's friends.

Someone told her Dave had left town. She heard he got a girl pregnant. She didn't ever find out who the girl was, although she thought about calling her up and asking her if it was true and telling her she was sorry—but she knew she'd never do that. She knew now she could have been the one who got pregnant. When she was going with Dave, she never really thought much about getting pregnant. Now she realized she should have.

Michelle was the only one she had talked to about what had happened with Dave. She didn't feel as if she could tell her parents. She knew they would be really hurt. Michelle said she should talk to the bishop, but she couldn't see doing that. The past was her secret, and it was better to keep it that way.

There were times when she felt good, when she enjoyed the protection the Church had to offer her from the rest of the world, when she liked being with Michelle and Elliott, when she felt that God wasn't mad at her anymore.

But at other times she wished some other guy would come into her life, times when she was lonely and wanted to be held in somebody's arms. At times like that she felt like an imposter, someone who wrestled with secret temptations but who looked and dressed and talked as much as possible as Michelle did.

It was so hard to be perfect, to do all the things members of the Church were supposed to do, to stay away from temptation. It was hard not to think about some things when she watched movies.

Sitting there listening to the others bear their testimonies, she thought, *I'm not one of them, not really, not anymore, maybe not ever.*

She knew she would have to get up and say something, but she didn't know what to say. She listened to what Angela was saying and decided to say some of the same things so nobody would know she didn't belong.

As others got up and bore their testimonies, Elliott thought about getting up and saying something. He looked over at Michelle. She noticed and smiled back at him. *She's so beautiful,* he thought. *I'm lucky to have her for my friend.*

He saw Michelle every day in orchestra. For him she was like rain in the desert and filled him with more self-confidence.

Two weeks earlier the orchestra and chorus had traveled to Idaho Falls to play at a music convention. It was a long trip. Michelle had sat with him both ways.

He had brought his latest copy of a computer magazine.

She grabbed it out of his hand and accused him of trying to show off how smart he was by bringing it on the bus.

"I don't have to show how smart I am because it's so obvious," he said.

She hit him over the head with the magazine. He grabbed her shoe and slid it down the aisle of the bus. "Elliott," she warned.

Mr. Kelly, the orchestra instructor, turned around and told Elliott to settle down.

Elliott beamed.

"What?" she asked him.

"This is the first time anyone's ever told me to settle down. Thank you, Michelle."

She laughed. "Anytime."

On the way back, late at night, she fell asleep and without knowing it leaned her head on his shoulder. It made him feel somehow responsible for her, although he couldn't think of any occasion when she would need him to protect her while she was sleeping.

When she woke up, she was a little embarrassed. "Sorry for using you as a pillow."

"You can do it anytime you want."

"Thanks. I might take you up on that sometime." She looked around. "Looks like most everybody else is asleep."

"Yeah, pretty much."

"Elliott, thanks for being a nice guy. Orchestra wouldn't be half as much fun without you."

"It's the same with me." He cleared his throat. "I'll never be able to tell you all you've done for me."

"Like what?"

"You've helped me know that there's more to life than being clever. I like to smell your perfume when we're near each other. You touch me on the shoulder to get my attention. You get mad at me when I do dumb things. You make church activities fun. You help me live the way I should." He paused. "I guess that's about it."

"We're friends, Elliott. That's what friends do—they help each other out."

It had been a wonderful trip. Now he looked around and realized it was his turn to say something. He stood up. "I don't have much to say . . . except how glad I am to have you all for my friends . . . especially Michelle. I think God couldn't be around to help me in high school, so he sent me Michelle to be my friend."

During the testimony meeting Michelle thought back to the girls' camp when she had committed once and for all to live the teachings of the Church. *I'm doing okay so far,* she thought. *Of course, it's not like I've had a lot of temptation. The only boy I've spent much time with is Elliott. He's turning into a nice guy and we have fun together, but he's not the one I'm looking for, not the one I'll marry someday.*

She looked around the room. *I wonder where he is.*

6

March 1986: Shane at Eighteen

"We need to go talk to the bishop," Jennifer said as Shane drove her home from their date.

"What for? Just because I brought a stupid blanket?"

"That's not the only reason. Bringing the blanket just made me realize that we're going to get into trouble if things keep going the way they've been going."

"We didn't do anything wrong. All I said was I thought it would be nice to lie down on the blanket and look at the stars."

"When have we ever looked at the stars when we've been up here?" she asked.

"Don't go to the bishop," he said.

"I'm going. Are you coming with me or not?"

"No."

"Fine, be that way then."

He took her home. They didn't say much at the door.

At home, on his way to his room, he knocked quietly on his parents' bedroom door. His mother invited him in.

"I'm home."

"Did you have a good time?"

"Yes."

"That's nice, dear."

"Well, good night."

59

"Good night, dear. Don't forget to turn out all the lights before you go to bed."

He went back to his room and lay down on the bed. He couldn't sleep. He wasn't sure how any of this had come about. After his experience with Gina, he had been so proud of himself that he had overcome temptation. He even told his bishop about the experience when he was interviewed. He was proud he had decided to live the standards of the Church.

After that, he expected that temptation would always come as it had with Gina, a clear and unmistakable invitation to do wrong. He was certain he could withstand a temptation like that if it ever came again.

And then, after years of being friends, he finally started dating Jennifer. She was everything he wanted a girl to be, and besides that, they were best friends.

They started as friends but gradually things changed. It wasn't until they had been going together for a while that he kissed her. After that, a good-night kiss became a regular part of their time together.

One time after a movie he drove to a place overlooking the town, a spot that few people ever came to. He turned off the motor and they kissed several times. Then he took her home. After that, they came up to the overlook after every date.

Gradually their kisses became longer and more passionate. No matter how many times he kissed her, it was never enough. He always wanted more.

It had all been so gradual that there was never a point at which he could say that what they were doing was wrong. He still thought of himself as being morally clean. And yet, he knew how he felt in the heat of their passion, and it was impossible to deny that there was a point when they were kissing that he thought about doing things he'd never done before.

He usually drove his dad's car when he took Jennifer out on a date. It was a Honda with bucket seats and manual trans-

mission, not the most convenient car for dating. He kept thinking that it would be more comfortable, when they went to the
overlook, to have a blanket so they could sit on the ground
with their backs against a tree and kiss. At first he hadn't brought
a blanket because he didn't know how he would explain it if
his parents or his sister saw him carrying one out to the car.
But tonight he had managed to take one out while the others
were watching a TV show in the family room.

That night they had started to kiss. After several long, passionate kisses, he suggested that they get out of the car. He
opened the door for her, took her hand, and walked hand in
hand with her to a nearby stand of trees.

"Let's sit down here," he said.

They sat down and he kissed her several times. Then he
went back to the car and got the blanket and brought it back
and spread it down on the ground. "We'll be more comfortable
now," he said.

"I think you'd better take me home," she said abruptly.

She walked to the car and got in. He picked up the blanket
and followed her, then started the motor. That's when she
suggested that they go talk to the bishop.

Shane felt that they didn't really need to bother the bishop
with something like this. They hadn't done anything wrong.
Couldn't they just not go to the overlook anymore? That would
solve the problem.

He didn't like the thought that the bishop might want more
details, and that they would have to tell him whatever he asked
about their relationship. The bishop would probably give them
some counsel, and sometime later he would want to know
how they were doing. Maybe he would suggest that they quit
seeing each other for a while. Shane didn't want that to happen.

The most amazing thing about this was that it had happened
so gradually. It wasn't like with Gina, where the invitation to
do wrong was obvious. This was much more subtle, much

more difficult to know when to sound the alarm within his mind.

Suddenly he thought of a trip he and his family had taken a few years earlier to a lake. It was a cold day, and Shane was the only one who wanted to go swimming. He walked into the shallow water near the shore. At first the water felt very cold to his feet and ankles, but eventually it didn't feel so cold. Then he walked out a little further, and the water felt cold to his legs up to his knees. But after a while that part of his body got used to the cold.

That's what happens, he thought. *We get used to some things, so that what used to be enough now isn't anymore.*

The strange thing about all this is that he and Jennifer didn't talk about it. What they did at the overlook was to each of them like something they did with a stranger. He wasn't sure why. Maybe if they could talk about it, they would realize that what they had been doing wasn't what they should have been doing.

He knew he would never be able to talk Jennifer out of going to see the bishop. And if he didn't go with her, then the bishop would call him in anyway, so he might as well get it over with.

"What can I do for you two?" the bishop asked.

Shane had thought about this meeting for several days. He had decided that instead of letting Jennifer tell what was wrong, he would take the lead and do it.

"Jennifer and I have been kissing a lot lately," he began. "Maybe too much. We've been going to a place I know, up on the rimrocks, where you can see the town. We've been going there a lot lately, and, well, last night we got out of the car and sat down on the ground. After we'd kissed for a while, I thought . . . " He could feel the sweat beading up on his forehead. He cleared his throat. "I thought . . . uh . . . that we'd be more comfortable if we could . . . uh . . . sit down on the ground . . . so I went and got a blanket in the trunk. When I spread it out, Jennifer told me to take her home. And then she said we needed to come to talk to you."

"I see. Do you mind if I ask a few questions?"

"No."

The bishop, a gentle person, spoke softly. "Have you two had sexual intercourse?"

"No," Shane answered.

"Have you been involved in touching intimate parts of each other's bodies?"

"Sometimes when we kiss good night we hold each other very tight," Jennifer said. "Is that what you mean?"

"I was mainly referring to touching with your hands, but holding each other very tight might be something you should cut down on."

"Whatever we did that was wrong was my fault," Shane said.

"Why do you say that?" she asked.

He thought she'd be glad he'd said it. He could never figure girls out.

"Because it was my responsibility to make sure nothing wrong happened while we were together."

"It was my responsibility too," she said.

"Do you have any ideas how you could avoid problems like this in the future?" the bishop asked.

"Well, maybe we shouldn't kiss each other anymore," Jennifer said.

Shane shook his head. "I think that's going too far the other way."

"Bishop, what do you think?" Jennifer asked.

"Shane, why do you kiss Jennifer?" the bishop asked.

"I don't know. I guess to show her I like her."

"Is that the only reason?" the bishop asked.

"No." He paused. "I like kissing her."

"After two or three kisses do you ever feel like, there, that's all the kissing I want to do tonight?" the bishop asked.

"You want the truth?" Shane asked.

"Yes."

"I always want more."

"Jennifer, what about you?"

"Sometimes I don't want to stop either."

"But you have to stop sometime. You have to set limits," the bishop said.

"Or else we might go too far," Shane said.

"It can happen that way," the bishop said. "So what limits do you want to put on yourselves?"

"Maybe we could limit it to four kisses on the doorstep at the end of the date," Shane suggested.

"What do you think about that?" the bishop asked Jennifer.

"If we set a number, like four, then Shane will expect that every time. And sometimes I might not want to kiss him at all. So I don't think we should put a number on it, because I can just hear him saying he's got three more coming, and I don't want it to be like that. I'm not a kissing machine, Shane."

"I never said you were."

The bishop cleared his throat. "I'll let you two work out the details, but I think the idea here is that you agree beforehand what your limits are going to be and then you never cross over those limits. And if you start going beyond the limits you've set, please come in and we'll talk some more about it." The bishop stood up. "How are you feeling about this now, Shane?"

"It was hard for me to come and talk to you," Shane said.

"I'm sure it's not easy. But there's a lot worse things than going to a bishop and telling him what you've done wrong. I'm not here to condemn anyone. I'm here to help, and that's what I want to do if you'll let me."

On the way home neither one of them spoke. In front of

her house, he got out immediately and went around and opened the door for her.

"Thanks for coming with me," she said.

"Yeah, sure."

"Do you want to come out to the backyard?" she asked.

"What for?"

"We could play on my brother's jungle gym."

They ended up with Shane resting on the parallel bars and Jennifer on the swing.

"How come you're so quiet?" she said.

"I wasn't trying to get you to go all the way with me, Jennifer."

"I know that. Things just got a little out of control . . . for me too." She paused. "I talked to my mom about what happened. She thinks that maybe we shouldn't see so much of each other."

"You told your mother?"

"Yes. Shane, I think maybe she's right." She cleared her throat. "Let's try not being together for a while and see how it goes. Okay?"

He felt awful but he wasn't going to let her know. "Sure, whatever you say."

After he left Jennifer's, he drove to Matt's house and rang the doorbell. Matt was still up.

"What happened to you?" Matt asked when he saw Shane's expression.

"Jennifer just broke up with me."

"She finally told you that it's really me she likes, right?"

"Yeah, something like that."

"You want some nachos?"

"I guess so."

Matt's mother had gotten out of bed to see who was at the door that time of night.

"Mom, you remember Shane, don't you? He used to spend a lot of time here before he discovered girls."

"Hi, Shane. Do you think my son will ever discover girls?"

"I've discovered them," Matt said defensively. "The only problem is they haven't discovered me yet."

"If you wouldn't treat them like they were dumb, you'd probably have better luck."

"Girls *are* dumb, Mom."

"Careful, or you'll be cooking your own meals from now on."

"Girls are very smart—especially moms."

"That's better." She left them.

Matt fixed up a big plate of nachos and set it on the kitchen table. "So, why did she dump you?"

"For no reason."

"So that means you'll be spending more time around here, right?"

"Yeah, right."

"I'll tell my mom to keep us stocked with tortilla chips and cheese."

June 1986: Shane Graduates from High School

And then suddenly it was over. Shane never could remember what his high school commencement speaker said. All he could think about was walking across the stage and getting his diploma.

At last it was his turn. As his name was called, he heard Megan yell out, "All right, Shane!" He walked across the stage, shook hands with the principal and the president of the school board, and then went back to his chair.

That night his parents helped him give a party for all his friends from high school, at least the ones who didn't drink. Jennifer came. They had remained friends since they'd quit seeing each other. She planned to go to summer school in California.

The party was going strong for a while, and then about

66

two in the morning everyone started to get tired. His parents were still hanging in there, but just barely. Some people even went home, but Shane and Jennifer were determined to stick it out as long as they could. They decided to take a walk. She reached for his hand. "We've come a long ways together."

"Yeah, we have. You've really been important in my life."

"Hey, you were good for me too."

"I'm sorry, you know, about what happened."

"I know. Me too."

"What are we going to think when we see each other in the future?" he asked.

"What good friends we've been."

"Not about the other?"

"No, not about the other. When I think about you I want to remember the good times."

"Will you write me on my mission?"

"You know I will."

"If you're still around when I get back, I'll look you up."

"I'll still be around."

"I hope you are."

They turned around and headed back. They could hear music coming from his house.

"By September everyone will be gone. This is it . . . it's all over."

They stopped walking and he put his arm around her and hugged her.

"Thank you for being my friend," she said.

"Thank you for being my friend," he repeated, too tired to be original.

By three in the morning everyone had gone home. He went out to the backyard and lay down on the trampoline and looked up at the stars. Just before falling asleep he thought to himself, *So this is what it's like to graduate from high school.*

When he woke up, it was quiet. The party was over. The class of 1986 was now history; suddenly he was an adult.

7

October 1986: Debra and Michelle at Sixteen

At midnight on the day of her sixteenth birthday, Michelle returned from her first official date.

"Did you have a good time?" her mother asked.

"It was just Elliott, Mom. Sometimes I feel like I've taken him on as a project — 'That's right, friends, send to the Help Make Elliott Human Foundation . . . so that someday he'll be able to find a wife.' I'm serious, Mom. He's like a kit you put together. I want a thank-you card from whoever marries him."

"What did he do wrong tonight?"

"He's been watching David Letterman. And so in the line for tickets he goes into this thing, like he was on late-night TV, and people look at him like he was crazy, and then they look at me, and I can see the pity in their eyes. And then during the movie, he's going, 'That could never happen . . . not in a million years . . . ' until somebody leans over and tells him to be quiet so people can enjoy the movie. Why me? You were right, Mom, we should've gone as a group — a very large group, like the entire school. Well, good night."

Inside her room, Michelle looked across the yard and saw that all the lights in Debra's house were off. She got ready for bed and turned off the light. But she wasn't sleepy, so she sat by the window and dreamed about a guy who wouldn't describe to her in vivid detail how bad his sinuses get in the winter.

Suddenly she noticed a figure coming out of Debra's house. At first she thought it was a burglar. She looked more closely. It was Debra, who walked out to the sidewalk and kept going.

Michelle put on shoes and a coat and went outside. Debra was standing on the corner waiting. Then a car pulled up and Debra got in. The car drove off.

As Michelle stepped inside the house, her mother was standing there waiting for her.

"Why did you go outside?"

"Debra just left in a car."

"Why?"

"I don't know why."

"Are you going to call her parents?"

"No."

"I think you should."

"She wouldn't want me to say anything."

"Her parents have a right to know what's going on."

"I won't tell on her."

"Then I will," her mother said, going to the phone.

January 1987: Debra at Muddy Gap, Wyoming

Debra sat in the drafty school bus and watched the endless fields of snow pass by. The wind was threatening to drift shut the county road that led to her uncle and aunt's place. They lived at the end of the line for the school bus.

Her parents had sent her to live with her uncle and aunt after she'd been caught coming home at three in the morning, back from the apartment of a guy she'd met at her after-school job. "You don't leave us much choice," her dad had said. "We need to send you someplace where you won't get into any trouble. I'm taking you to stay with Uncle John and Aunt Ruby."

It might as well have been the end of the world. They lived

so far from any town that you couldn't distinguish the many ghosts on the TV picture from the real picture, but her uncle and aunt didn't believe in satellite dishes. They believed in hard work during the day and reading scriptures after evening chores were done.

Twice a month they went into town for supplies. The school she went to had all the grades from seventh grade through twelfth grade in one building. There were fifteen people her age, eight of them girls. Of the seven boys, none had any interest in her, and even if they had, she wouldn't have been interested in them.

Her parents wrote once a week. "I hope you understand we did this because we love you," her father wrote one time. She wrote back, "You have a strange way of showing love."

Michelle wrote often, mostly with news about her friends in high school. Angela was moving with her parents to Eugene, Oregon, at the end of the school year. Elliott had been selected to go to Washington, D.C., for a math competition.

The bus stopped and the Ferguson boys got off. Debra was the only one left.

"Might as well come up and talk to me," the driver said.

She picked up her books, walked to the front of the bus, and sat down.

The driver, Larry, was in his twenties. In high school he had been a basketball star, but now he was driving a school bus.

"I've heard you're kind of wild and that's why your folks sent you here," he said. "Is that true?" He looked at her and smiled. It was a smile she'd come to recognize, and it was here, even in the middle of nowhere, a smile that needed to be reckoned with and decided upon.

Trying to be perfect had never worked with her. She didn't know why exactly, except she knew she wasn't a good person, and no matter how hard she tried, it was just a matter of time until she slipped up again. Being with a guy wasn't all that

70

great, but it was better than the emptiness she felt when she was alone. What good did it do to keep pretending to be something she wasn't? She wasn't like Michelle and she never would be.

How strange that even in the middle of nowhere she could come up with guys who wanted to treat her the way all the guys she'd ever known had treated her. *What is it about me?* she thought. It couldn't be what she was wearing. She wore flannel shirts and jeans to school, just like everybody else. It couldn't be anything she could think of, except maybe the way she looked at a guy when she caught him staring at her.

He wanted an answer to his question. "Do you think I could be wild?" she said.

"Yeah, I think so. Do you want to stop and talk? I know a place where we could park this thing and nobody'd see it."

"No thanks."

"If you ever change your mind, let me know."

"I won't change my mind."

"You might. It's a long winter."

"Not that long."

"Suit yourself. I'll always be here . . . every day."

I won't, she thought.

That was the day she made plans to run away.

June 1987: Shane at Nineteen

For some reason Shane's sister, Megan, decided that his farewell should be a roast. She began her talk with, "First of all, looking at all these people who came here today, I can't decide if it's because they want to show their support, or if it's because they want to make sure you leave town."

"Seriously, I have a lot of reasons to be glad Shane is going on a mission, but the main reason is I get his leather jacket while he's gone.

"Growing up with Shane as a big brother hasn't been easy. Sometimes we've really fought like crazy. People talk about girls spending a lot of time in the bathroom but let me tell you, Shane tops them all. And another thing, he used to get so mad at me when I'd wear his clothes. I don't see what the big deal was. I offered to let him wear mine—but he never did.

"Okay, this is the serious part. Shane has always been a good example for me. Like there was one time when this girl really liked Shane—Jennifer, it was before you—I mean, like this girl was crazy for Shane, or maybe just crazy, I'm not sure which. Anyway, Shane didn't give in to temptation, and that really impressed me, and I just want you to know, Shane, that your example has helped me a lot. I just want to say that I'm proud of you for wanting to serve a mission, and I'll write and send you cookies, mostly the batches that don't turn out. Seriously, I'll send a few good ones too, especially if you show all your companions my picture and tell them what a wonderful person I am and that I'll be at BYU about the time they get back from their missions." She turned to face him. "I love you, big guy. Thanks for being such a good big brother to me."

April 1988, letter from Jennifer to Shane:

Dear Shane,

This is the hardest letter I've ever had to write but I've known for some time now that I needed to let you know what is going on.

You remember me writing and telling you about Steve? Well, I've fallen in love with him. He's asked me to marry him and I've told him I would.

I know this comes as kind of a shock to you, but it's a surprise to me too, because I didn't think it would ever happen. I want to thank you for being such a good friend to me all the way through high school. You were always someone I looked up to. You made it easy for me to live the gospel and I want to thank you for that.

We will always be a part of each other because of the experiences we had together. I'm proud of you for serving a mission and I'll continue to pray for your success just like I've done all along. And I'll be sure and send you a wedding announcement. Steve and I plan on being married this summer.

Love,
Jennifer

April 1988, letter from Matt to Shane:

Shane,

So Jennifer dumped you, right? If she was going to do it, I hoped she'd leave you for me, but no. She has to go for another Mormon. What's wrong with Lutherans anyway?

So, how are you doing? Things are kind of boring here at college. I wish you were here. The people around here have never seen the Dynamic Duo in action.

Do you like being a missionary? If so, why? Let me know, okay?

Matt, the Man of La Macho

April 1988, letter from Megan to Shane:

Elder Shane,

This new companion of yours, have you shown him my picture yet? I keep telling you to have kind of a shrine to me on the top of your dresser.

Sorry about you and Jennifer, but I can't say I'm surprised. She knew you before you quit cracking your knuckles. What you need is a girl who didn't know you in high school. I bet you'll find someone at the Y after your mission.

You asked about your leather jacket. No, I haven't lost it yet. I'm very careful with it actually. Your stereo is junk now though, but don't worry about it. You can always get a job and get yourself a new one.

I've been trying to do what you said about dating but it's kind of hard here. There's not that many LDS guys around, you know, and what there are, my age, are about as mature as a duck. But the last couple of times we've done things as a group like you said.

I went in your room the other day and just sat there and remembered what it was like with you around. I miss you, I really do. I never thought I'd say that. Be good,

Megan

February 1988: Michelle, a Senior in High School

At two in the morning the phone rang. Michelle picked it up on the second ring.

"Didn't wake you up, did I?" Debra teased.

"Debra, where are you?"

"In Colorado. Don't tell my parents, okay?"

"Okay. They've really been worried about you. What are you doing for money?"

"I work at a ski resort. I'm one of the ski instructors."

"Do your mom and dad know where you're at?"

"No. Don't tell 'em either, okay?"

"Can I tell 'em you're all right?"

"Yeah, sure."

"Are you going to school?"

"No, but I'm going to get my G.E.D. Chuck says I've got to at least have that."

"Who's Chuck?"

"The guy I'm staying with. He's a ski instructor too."

"Do you ever go to church?"

"No, not anymore."

"Your mom and dad are really worried about you."

"Tell 'em not to worry. Actually it's real nice here. Remember Sister Drummond telling us to look for wildlife? Well, she'd go crazy here."

"We're so far apart anymore."

"I know. You getting all set to graduate?"

"There's not much to do to get ready. You just have to keep going to classes."

"How's Elliott?"

"He's doing good. What's Chuck like?"

"He's okay most of the time. I don't have much to complain about with him." There was a long pause. "I suppose you're going to college in September, right?"

"I'm going to BYU."

"That's the one thing I regret . . . well, there's a lot of things actually, but that's the main thing. As soon as I can save up some money, I want to maybe come home and go to the U. I won't stay with my parents, that's for sure. Michelle, I think about you a lot—more than anybody else actually. You remember that time in the canoe?"

"I remember. Can I do anything for you?"

"Well, not much. I guess you could pray for me."

"I do that already."

"Well, good. Maybe that's why my life isn't more messed up than it is. Look, Chuck is getting mad 'cause I'm running up his phone bill. See you around someday, okay?"

"Okay."

Michelle hung up the phone and went to the window and looked across the yard to the house where Debra's parents lived. One light was still on. She'd seen it on before late at night. She asked her mother about it once and was told, "They're having a tough time, not knowing where Debra is or if she's even alive."

She put on a robe and socks and boots and a coat and ran across the field of snow that separated their houses. She knocked on the door.

When Debra's mother came to the door, Michelle realized

she had halfway thought it might be Debra coming home. She opened the door and saw that it was just Michelle.

"I just heard from Debra."

"Please come in."

Debra stood at the window and watched it snow. Tomorrow would be a busy day.

Most of the things she'd told Michelle were true. She was in Colorado at a ski resort and she was living with a guy named Chuck. But she wasn't a ski instructor; she washed dishes in the ski lodge. Chuck was a ski instructor though. He'd been her instructor on one of her days off. He liked to flirt with the women in his group, and on that day it was her. She moved in with him a week later.

And now every day, while she worked in the kitchen, he was out on the slopes smiling and winking and joking with women who were either older but very rich or not so rich but very beautiful.

Sometimes he didn't come home at night. She didn't complain as much as she should have because she had nowhere else to go. And besides, the rich women and the beautiful girls only stayed a week at most, and then they were gone and Chuck came back.

Why is it, she thought, *that no matter where I go or what I do, I end up feeling trapped?*

She closed her eyes. *Oh, Michelle, please keep praying for me.*

8

December 1989: Shane and Michelle at BYU

After being released from his mission in June, Shane worked two months, then began fall semester at Brigham Young University. Because funds were tight, he got a part-time job in the BYU Bookstore. After his finals were over, he agreed to stay on to work until December 23; then he would drive home.

On December 22 things would ordinarily be slow with most of the students gone, but that day the store was especially quiet because it was snowing so hard. His boss called to say he couldn't get to work because of the weather.

Shane worked in men's clothing. Across a wide aisle, in women's clothing, was a girl he'd always wanted to meet. He'd seen her a couple of times, but they had always seemed to be working different shifts throughout most of the semester.

With practically no customers in the store, it was inevitable that Shane and Michelle should end up facing each other.

"Not much to do today, is there," she said.

"Not much." He found himself staring at her. She had dark brown hair and a tan complexion, which he at first suspected came from sitting under a sunlamp but later learned was her natural coloring.

She was very much aware of the way he was looking at her, but it didn't matter because she was looking at him too.

"It'd be a good day to go skiing," he said. "Do you ski?"

"No, not really."

"Want to learn sometime?" he asked.

"If I went, I'd probably break my leg."

"No, you wouldn't. The important thing is to take a lesson. Never let anyone take you who says, 'Oh, I'll show you how to ski.' Because they'll get you to the top of the mountain, give you five minutes of not very helpful hints, and then abandon you. It'll be you against the mountain, and the mountain will win. But if you take a lesson, at the end of two hours you'll know how to turn and you'll know how to stop." He paused. "In skiing those are very important things to know."

"I have a friend who's a ski instructor in Colorado." She paused. "Maybe you're right, maybe I should learn how to ski."

"You might as well. I mean, after all, thousands of people come to Utah from all over the world to ski, and for us it's just a few minutes away. So, you want to go with me sometime?"

"Yes."

He felt comfortable around her, as if he'd known her a long time. He crossed the aisle to be closer to her. "You didn't go home for Christmas either?" he asked.

"Well, actually I live in Salt Lake. What about you?"

"I'm from Montana but I wanted to work to save up some money for next semester. My plan was to drive home tomorrow, but now with all this snow, I'm not sure that's such a good idea. They say the interstate up through Idaho is closed."

"Did all your roommates go home for Christmas?"

"Yes."

"So you're all alone?"

"Yeah, but it's not so bad. At least I don't have to yell for somebody to turn down the music."

"If you have to stay here for Christmas, do you have anywhere to go?" she asked.

"I haven't worried much about that."

"Why don't you come to our place? We'll have a full house

anyway. My brothers' and sister's families will all be there. So if you like lots of kids and noise and confusion . . . "

"Yeah, I do."

"Me too."

He had the vague feeling that somewhere the two of them had practiced what they were saying now. He felt as if he could tell her anything and she'd understand, that he knew her life story, and that she knew his.

"On Christmas Eve if you have things that need putting together, I'm very good at that."

"My dad'll be happy to hear that. If you want, you could come over Christmas Eve and help and then stay in our guest room for the night."

For anyone else he would have said, "I don't want to be in the way," but he didn't say it to her because he knew he wouldn't be in the way. He knew he'd fit in and the two of them would enjoy being together for Christmas.

"Thanks. I'd like that."

They stopped talking and just looked at each other. At first she was self-conscious and flashed a nervous smile, but then it passed, and she quit questioning what it meant and they both just enjoyed the experience.

Finally he spoke. "You know what, if I were going to do a TV ad for Nuts, Raisin, and Fiber Cereal, I'd show you in a sunny field picking grapes."

She smiled. "You think I'd make a good migrant worker, is that what you're saying?"

"I'm sure you'd be good at anything you tried. Are you sure you'll have enough room for me with all your family home for the holidays?"

"Yes. We have a big house. There's plenty of room."

They talked for three hours and then ate lunch together and talked and then returned to work and talked some more. When he asked how she was getting home, she said that because of the weather she was taking the bus that day, so he offered to drive her home.

The interstate was snow-packed and slippery, but he'd had a lot of experience driving in snow in Montana, so they took it easy and talked. Before long they pulled into her driveway and she invited him in for supper. He met her parents and then they ate. The two of them volunteered to do the dishes. They talked while they worked and then sat down at the kitchen table and talked some more.

By ten thirty they were both tired, but neither one wanted the night to end so they stalled. He said "Well, I'd better be going" ten times before she got his coat from the closet.

"I like your leather jacket," she said.

"Here, put it on." He helped her on with it. "Oh, look if it smells of perfume, don't blame me. My sister wore it all during my mission."

She took a deep breath. "I've always liked the smell of leather."

"Yeah, me too."

They ran out of words at the door and just looked at each other. Neither one wanted to put words to what was happening. To say "I don't know why we keep looking at each other" would have betrayed whatever it was that was happening.

"I feel like I've known you all my life but I just didn't know it," he said.

She smiled. "I feel the same way."

Her father came out and said, "Michelle, it's late."

Having her father do that embarrassed her. After all, she was in college now, so to be treated as if she were still in high school seemed out of place, but it did the job her father intended. Shane left the house.

In the driveway he had to brush the accumulated snow off his car. As he was doing so, he looked toward the house. The front door was still open, and Michelle was watching him through the storm door. He stopped working and waved to

80

her. She waved back. He ran over to the middle of the lawn and fell down backwards into the snow and moved his arms and made an angel in the snow and then stood up and bowed. She flicked the porch light twice as a silent applause. He made a snowball and lobbed it at the front door. It landed with a soft thud. Then he turned to finish cleaning the snow off his car. Suddenly he was startled by the thud of a snowball on the hood. He turned and there she was in a coat and boots.

"You missed me," he said.

"I missed you on purpose. Next time you won't be so lucky."

"Yeah, right." He continued brushing snow off the car.

A snowball hit him in the back. She started giggling, as surprised as he was that she'd managed to hit him.

He turned. "Well, I see I have some unfinished business here."

"Shane, don't."

He picked her up in his arms and dropped her screaming into the deepest snowdrift he could find.

As he returned to scrape the windows of his car, she came up behind him and dropped some snow down his neck. He turned and pulled her down into the snow with him. She scooped up some snow and tried to toss it in his face but he grabbed her arm.

And then the world slowed down and stopped. Clocks around the world quit ticking and planes froze in midair. It was just the two of them, looking at each other, and for a brief instant not even snow was cold anymore.

The porch light flicked on and her father, now in robe and pajamas, stepped outside. "Michelle, the neighbors are trying to sleep. Please show a little consideration for others."

"Let's get him," Michelle whispered.

They grabbed some snow and chased her father inside.

"I don't want this night to ever end," she said.

"Me either."

"Why is everyone sleeping when the snow is so beautiful?"

"People with house payments are like that."

Her father, standing inside the door, flicked the light on and off several times.

"I'd better go," Shane said.

They stood up and brushed themselves off, and then she walked him to his car.

"I'm usually very responsible," she said. "When I was growing up, I was the kind of person other parents wished their child was like."

"I believe that."

"See that house? My friend Debra used to live there. If she were here, she'd come out and play with us."

"Where is she now?"

"I don't know. Last I heard she was in Colorado at a ski resort. Nobody knows. It's a long story. Would you like to come in for some hot chocolate?"

"Your parents have already gotten rid of me once tonight. I'd better go."

"Will I see you tomorrow?" she asked.

"Yes, at work—and later too, if that's okay with you."

"Do you remember the first time you tasted chocolate?" she asked.

"Not really."

"I do. This reminds me of that."

Because of the weather it took him much longer than usual to drive back to Provo. As he was getting ready for bed, the phone rang. He picked it up.

"I was just wondering if you made it home okay," she said.

"Yes."

"I was worried. I should have asked you to stay the night in our guest room."

"Will you be able to make it to work in the morning?"

"I think so, if the bus is running. They say it's going to let up. How about you?"

"I'll be there."

"Well, I suppose I should let you get some sleep," she said.

"I'm not sleepy."

"Me neither. I have a phone in my room, so we could talk, if you want to."

"Sure."

"You remember me telling you about the girl who lived next door? Well, we used to talk late at night on the phone." She paused. "Let's start at the beginning," she said, "how it was for you when you were born."

"I was born at an early age," he said.

They traded grade school experiences and then worked into junior high and then high school. When it came time to finally say good night, he wanted to say how he felt about her but he didn't know what to say. To say "I love you" didn't seem right for only having known her one day, and, besides, it wasn't that exactly. It was something else—the feeling she was somehow a part of him that he'd lost long ago and had been looking for all these years.

"I feel like I've known you for a long time," he said.

"I feel the same way."

"Strange, isn't it?"

"Yes, but very nice."

During a break the next day at work, he approached the counter where she was working. "I'm here on business."

"I see. And how may I help you?"

"I need to buy a Christmas present for a girl."

A little unsure of who the gift was for, Michelle at first proceeded cautiously. "Do you have anything in mind?"

"Not really. What do you think would be good?"

"What size is she?"

"She's about your size."

She smiled. "Color of hair?"

"It's the same as yours."

"Really?"

"Yes."

"I don't think you need to buy this girl a Christmas present."

"Why not?"

"Because you're working to save up money for books and tuition, not for Christmas presents."

"But I want to show this girl that I . . . " He paused. "That I like her a lot."

"She probably already knows that."

"Still, I want to get her something for Christmas."

"I think I can help you. Please follow me."

She led him to the school supplies section, picked up a box of paper clips, and gave it to him. "Give this to your friend. It has many uses. You can make a necklace or a bracelet or you can unbend one of 'em and make the letter S."

"What does the letter S stand for?"

"At Christmastime it could stand for Santa. By the way, did you know that Rudolph the Red-nosed Reindeer is getting so old that his nose won't light up anymore so Santa has to jump-start him every Christmas Eve? A friend of mine told me that once. His name's Elliott, and he can be really funny sometimes. He's on a mission now." She paused, then added, "He and I are just friends."

He bought the box of paper clips. It cost him eighty-nine cents.

On Christmas Eve he arrived at her house in the late afternoon. As Michelle had warned him, the house was full of people. Two of her brothers and her sister were married with kids of their own.

When supper was ready, Shane and Michelle volunteered to eat with the little kids. They ate in the playroom. Shane liked kids, and more than anything liked to make them laugh. By the end of the evening he and Michelle couldn't have a minute to themselves without having children wanting to play with them.

At about nine o'clock the parents tried to get their children to go to bed and to sleep so they could start their preparations for Christmas, but the kids were too excited. As soon as the adults thought they were all down for the night, one or more of the kids would turn up in the living room saying they couldn't sleep. And so it wasn't until after eleven o'clock that the work of assembling the toys began.

Shane and Michelle were assigned to put together one bicycle, two tricycles, and one set of hot wheels. They made a good team. Michelle would inventory the parts and read the directions, while Shane looked at the drawings and decided how the parts fit together. Between the two of them, they were able to figure out even the most poorly worded directions.

Finally at one fifteen they were the only ones still up. They finished the last tricycle they had been working on and stood up. Shane's legs hurt because he'd been sitting on the floor for so long.

"I'll show you where the guest bedroom is," she said.

It was down the hall. She flicked on the lights only to discover that one of her brothers and his wife had taken over that room.

"Sorry," she said, shutting the door. "They were supposed to sleep downstairs in my room. Well, let's go downstairs and see what's available there."

She tried a room in the basement, but it was occupied too.

"I know there's a place for you somewhere," she said.

"The garage, right?"

"You wouldn't mind, would you? We could make room for you between the lawn mower and the snow blower. Just kidding. You can stay in my room if you want, and I'll sleep in a sleeping bag on the couch in the family room."

"I'll take the couch."

"I feel awful about this — asking you to stay over and then

85

not having a place for you to sleep. We figured this all out before you came, but somehow it got mixed up."

"Don't worry. I'll be fine. We'd better get some sleep now. Merry Christmas."

"Merry Christmas."

He reached in his coat pocket and brought out a small present.

"You might as well open this now."

On his lunch hour the day before he had taken one of the paper clips, bent it out in the shape of an S, then asked a jeweler to attach a gold chain in order to make it into a necklace.

She unwrapped it. "Shane, I didn't want you to spend your money on me. It's beautiful. Thank you very much."

"S is for sharing," he said.

"Thank you. I love it." She kissed him on the cheek and then said, "I have a present for you too. I'll be right back." She brought back an envelope wrapped in Christmas ribbon. He opened it. Inside was a gift certificate for two for skiing.

"Now you'll have to take me skiing," she said.

"This cost a lot more than what I spent."

"It's not only from me. It's from my parents too."

To Shane it felt as if he'd slept maybe half an hour when he heard little voices, excitedly opening presents in the living room down the hall.

He slept off and on through the noise, but then he heard Michelle's voice. "Oh, look what Santa brought me," she said, coming into the family room and playfully running her fingers through his hair. "I wonder if it's battery operated or if you wind it up."

Still in the sleeping bag, he sat up.

"Oh, look, it moves," Michelle teased. "Not very fast, but it does move."

She left while he went into the guest bathroom to get

dressed. Then he joined her and the rest of the family to see and play with the kids' toys. Then they all had a hearty breakfast, eating whatever they wanted with no thought of calories or cutting down. After all, it was Christmas.

After breakfast Michelle and Shane volunteered to do the dishes. After they finished, she got the scrapbook of her life and let him look through it.

"Who's this other girl in all the pictures?"

"That's Debra, the girl I told you about who lived next door. She's beautiful, isn't she?"

"Yes, but so are you."

"Thank you."

"You played the cello?"

"Yes, I played it in high school."

"Do you still play?"

"A little."

"I want a concert from you today."

"No you don't. I haven't practiced for a long time."

"Don't get shy on me all of a sudden."

"And what will you do for me?"

"Well, I played football in high school, so I could run out for a pass."

"That'd fit right in with all the other commotion we've got here today."

"Let's hear you on the cello now, okay?"

She went to her room and got the instrument, then played him a song. He said it was good.

"Not really, but that's not the point. The point is that in high school this gave me an identity, and it showed me I had talents, and it built my self-esteem, so if I never play another note, it was worth it."

"That's sort of what football gave me."

By eleven all the kids were tired since they'd gotten up so early. "C'mon, kids, let's go take a nap," Michelle said. "Uncle Shane and I will take a nap with you guys, okay?"

They turned the TV on and lay down on the family room floor. The younger ones wanted to be lying next to either Shane or Michelle.

"Has everyone gone potty?" Michelle asked.

Shane, a little embarrassed, was the only one to get up and go into the bathroom. By the time he got back, almost everyone was asleep. He reclaimed his position next to Michelle and lay down. Because she was awake, they lay there and talked.

"Debra and I used to talk like this at girls' camp."

Eventually they both slept until it was time for lunch.

In the afternoon he called his family. He had each of them talk to Michelle. He talked last to Megan.

"Say yes if you think this thing with Michelle might get serious," she said.

"Yes."

"That's what I thought. Another one bites the dust, hey?"

That night, back again in his lonely apartment, he realized that when they were together it was like they were both in a trance because they said things that made sense then, but afterwards those same things seemed out of place. When they were sitting on the floor playing with her nieces and nephews, he had talked about their being married and having kids of their own, yet he'd never asked her to marry him. It was as if they both just accepted the fact that it was going to happen.

But these dream-world feelings couldn't go on forever. At some point the logical part of their brains had to catch on to what was going on intuitively.

It happened the day after classes started. "I think we'd better not see each other for a while," she said.

"Why do you think that?"

"Everything's been going too fast. I just need some time to think."

"All right, fine, whatever you want. Let me know when you're ready to start seeing me again."

She later confessed that she felt totally depressed because he took her suggestion so easily. She told him she cried after he left.

He thought being away from her would help him get organized as far as his classes went, but it didn't. He found himself staring into space instead of studying.

After one week she telephoned. "You promised to take me skiing. Is that still a possibility?"

"Yes, of course."

The next Saturday they went. In the morning she took a two-hour lesson while he skied by himself. They ate lunch in the lodge and then decided to go on the bunny slope together.

"What if I fall when I get off the chair lift?" she asked.

"Look at yourself. You've got goggles and you've got a scarf around your face and a wool cap over your head. It's the perfect disguise. It doesn't matter if you mess up because nobody knows who you are. It's no big deal."

Once on top they proceeded slowly to the edge of the hill and looked down.

"This is too steep," she said.

"No it isn't. You can do it. Just do wedge turns back and forth, like you practiced in your lesson."

She thought about it. "I've never backed away from a challenge."

"I know. That's one of the things I like about you. Oh, by the way, I love you."

"Don't say things like that up here."

"I'm sorry. It was thoughtless of me." Their gaze locked in like a radar system.

"Don't, Shane. I'm going to need all my concentration just to make it down from here alive."

"You're right. We came here to ski. Come on, follow me."

He skied about thirty feet down the hill and then turned around and shouted directions for her until she made it to where he was.

"That's good, except for the fact you look like a comma on skis. This time bend your knees but not your back."

At first she fell a lot, but she always managed to get up again. He knew that with just a few days more on the slopes, she'd be skiing well enough to keep up with him. He also realized that what her past experiences had done for her was to give her the confidence that she could learn anything, master any situation, conquer any obstacle. And that's what he wanted in the woman who would one day become his wife. It wasn't that he had a checklist—just that sometimes he looked for reasons that would stand up in court for feeling about her the way he did.

At four o'clock they drove back to her parents' home in Salt Lake City. They were both exhausted from their day of skiing and ended up sitting on the couch in front of the TV, his arm around her shoulders, both of them asleep.

At ten thirty her mother came in the family room and told Michelle it was time for Shane to go.

They went into the living room, where her parents were starting to turn off the lights. Michelle's mother asked if they'd like some cookies and milk, but her father said, "It's time for Shane to leave. He's got a long drive home, and the roads aren't too good."

Shane put on his jacket, and Michelle walked him to the front door. He reached down and pointed to the lift ticket fastened onto the zipper of his jacket. "What you want to do is to keep your ticket on your jacket for as long as possible."

"Why's that?"

"Because then people you don't even know will come up to you and ask you if you ski, and you'll tell them yes, of course,

90

doesn't everyone? Off the slope nobody knows you're not an expert skier. So you might as well play the part, right?"

"You're a funny guy."

"On a more serious note, I think we should talk about getting married."

"You do?"

"Yes, don't you?"

"Yes."

"So . . . will you marry me?"

"Yes."

He didn't know what to say after that. She helped him out by kissing him.

Suddenly her father came into the hallway. "It's getting late, Michelle," he said.

"Dad, Shane just asked me to marry him and I said yes."

"He did? You did?"

"Yes."

"That's great news! Does your mother know yet?"

"No, not yet."

"Let's go tell her then."

The four of them had cookies and milk to celebrate. Just before Shane left, he said to Michelle, "Well, I guess I know how to get on your dad's good side, don't I? A proposal gets me an extra hour. What would I have to do to get to stay two extra hours?"

"Win the Nobel Peace Prize," she said.

The next Saturday Shane and Michelle went skiing again, then stopped at a restaurant for pizza. While they were waiting to be served at their table, Michelle suddenly stopped talking.

"What's wrong?" he asked.

"Just a minute. I think that's my friend Debra over there."

Debra was standing at the take-out counter.

Michelle walked over. "Debra, is that really you?"

"Michelle?"

The two girls hugged, practically collapsing with their delight, then came over to where Shane was. Michelle introduced her and they all sat down.

"What are you doing these days?" Michelle asked.

"Taking classes at the university and working part-time." She paused. "I wish Ryan were here so you could meet him."

"Ryan?" Michelle said. "What's he like?"

"Well, he's a financial planner but he's done a lot of work lately in state government. He's great looking and very smart, and he drives a Porsche."

"Sounds great," Michelle said. "Any plans for marriage?"

"No, not yet. Neither one of us is ready for that yet."

"Shane and I are getting married August 24. Will you be here then?"

"As far as I know."

"I want you to stand in the receiving line with me."

"Where's the reception going to be?"

"At the church."

"I doubt if you want me there."

"Of course I do."

"I'm not that terrific of a Mormon anymore. I've been disfellowshipped."

"What happened?"

"I was sort of lost as far as the church records go, but then finally they located me, and the bishop found out Ryan and I are living together, so he called me in to talk about it. He said it wasn't right but I told him it was right for me and I was going to stay with Ryan and it didn't matter what the Church thought about it. So it all ended up with me being disfellowshipped." She paused. "I wasn't going to church anyway. And Ryan and I are very happy together."

"I really do want you in the receiving line at my reception. You were my best friend all the way through school."

"I'll think about it."

92

"Let me get your phone number so I'll know how to reach you."

She gave Michelle her phone number.

"Do your folks have this number?" Michelle asked.

"No. We're not in contact much anymore. My dad's had a tough time accepting the way things have turned out." She looked at her watch. "Ryan's waiting for me to bring the pizza home, so I'd better go before he dies of starvation. Look, maybe the four of us could get together sometime. I think you'd really like Ryan."

"Sure, let's do that sometime."

9

February 17, 1990: Debra and Ryan

As Debra drove to the apartment where she and Ryan lived, she thought back to when she and Michelle had been so close. And yet if she had to do it all over again, she didn't think she would change anything. She had found a man she loved.

Ryan Baxter was a woman's dream come true — handsome, articulate, and admired by all who met him. He was born and raised in Boston. He did well in school and was valedictorian of his graduating class. Then he attended the University of California at Berkeley on a scholarship.

Debra, after working as a dishwasher the previous winter and a waitress during the summer, had finally realized her parents had been right after all — she needed to go to college. In August she had come home. She told her parents she was sorry for running away, announced that now she wanted to go to college, and asked them to help her pay for at least part of it. She made it clear she didn't intend to live at home or abide by their standards. They agreed to help out. She thanked them and told them where to send the checks, then went to see what she had to do to get accepted at the University of Utah.

She met Ryan in October at a panel discussion for a class she was taking. She was immediately impressed by his smooth, confident manner. Afterwards she walked up to him and told him his views about state aid to education were flawed. It was unusual for Ryan to meet anyone who could compete with him intellectually, but to have a beautiful young woman do it was even more rare. He asked her out to dinner that night.

A month later she moved into his apartment. She thought about keeping her old apartment because, although she seldom visited her parents, they did have her address. She didn't want them to know details about her private life, but she also realized that keeping her old apartment would cost her too much money, so one day she phoned her mother and told her the news. Her mother surprised her. Instead of condemning Debra, she said, "You must love him very much."

"Yes, I do."

"Then bring him home for us to meet."

She even did that once. But although her parents did their best to be warm and supportive, she felt that her father resented the fact that she'd gone against all she'd been taught.

Later she suspected her father contacted the bishop of the ward she lived in and told him what was going on, because two weeks later the bishop phoned and asked her to come in to see him. When she met with him, he asked if it was true she was living with a man outside of marriage. She said yes. He told her that what she was doing was a serious transgression, and she said she didn't think it was that serious because she and Ryan loved each other, and to her that was the most important thing.

She and the bishop talked a long time. She was proud that she could counter every argument he presented about why what she was doing was wrong. He used scriptures, but she said she didn't believe them anymore.

Finally he closed his books and said, "Your membership in the Church is at stake here."

"That's not as important to me as being with the man I love."

He paused. "Are you sure?"

"Yes, I'm sure."

"Then you leave me no choice. I will have to convene a disciplinary council."

"Do what you have to do. I think it'll be better for everyone concerned, don't you?"

A week later two somewhat shy and polite men appeared at her door. She invited them in, and they handed her a letter from the bishop. She read the letter. It was official notice of the date for the disciplinary council meeting.

"Tell the bishop I won't be coming," she said.

"Why not?" one of the men asked.

"Why put me or the bishop through what will essentially be a depressing experience?"

"Things would be better if you showed up," the other man said.

"In what way?"

"Someday you might want to come back to the Church."

"I don't think so." She stood up, and they got the hint it was time to leave.

One of the men had tears in his eyes as he paused at the door. "I know that the Church is true," he said.

"Yes, I suppose it is. It's just that I can't live the way members are supposed to live. I've tried and it never quite works out."

After they left, Ryan came out from the kitchen, where he'd been waiting for the visitors to leave. "What was that all about?" he asked.

"Nothing much," she said. "Nothing at all. Just some people from my church. But don't worry. They won't be coming back."

Not long after, she received official notice that she had been disfellowshipped.

Now, as she entered the apartment with the pizza, she found Ryan in a sweatsuit, riding an exercise bike and watching TV.

She found a spot on his cheek that wasn't sweaty and kissed him. "I'm back," she said.

"Something smells good."

"Is it me or the pizza?"

"The pizza."

"Have you got the mail yet?" she asked.

"No. I'll get it when my time's up."

"Don't bother. I can get it."

She went outside to the curb, where each tenant had a locked metal mail box. She opened their box and took out the mail. Then, standing next to a garbage can, she tossed out everything addressed to Occupant. No letter for her. She noticed an official-looking letter from the office of the governor of California. It was for Ryan. *I wonder what that's all about?* she thought.

Back in the apartment, she handed the letter to Ryan. She was curious about it but had learned that it was not a good idea to talk to him when he was exercising. She would ask him after he finished.

She made herself a cup of coffee. Since she'd been disfellowshipped from the Church, she realized there was no longer any reason to feel guilty about breaking the Word of Wisdom. She and Ryan enjoyed drinking coffee first thing in the morning and with dinner at night. She drank wine once in a while for social occasions but didn't like it all that much. She had never started smoking because it seemed like a dumb thing. With all the talk about air pollution, why make your own?

She couldn't help thinking about Michelle and Shane. They seemed so happy. She loved Ryan and she wouldn't trade what she had for anything, but sometimes she felt as if she'd missed out not having a wedding.

She remembered the night when she and Ryan decided to live together. There were no invitations sent out, no announcements in the newspaper, no wedding cake, no reception line where she could receive the greetings and blessings of all her friends and loved ones. All that happened was she and Ryan moved her things over to his place.

A few minutes later Ryan came in the kitchen. She turned on the microwave and heated up the pizza.

"What took you so long?" he asked.

"When I went to pick it up, I saw a girl there I grew up with. Her name's Michelle. I think I've told you about her before."

"Is she a Mormon?" he asked. He couldn't ask a question like that without some hint of ridicule in his voice.

"Yes. A good one though, not like me."

His mind did not do well with idle conversation. "Is there some point to this story?"

"Not really. It was just nice to see her again. What's your news from California?"

"Nothing much. It's just that I'm always looking around for new opportunities."

"So what's this about?"

"It's too early to say. I'll tell you if anything comes of it."

"I just want to know why you'd be getting a letter from the governor's office in California."

"There's an opening on the governor's staff. I've applied for it."

"Why didn't you tell me about it?"

"I don't think I should have to report to you everything I do."

"Can I read the letter?"

"No."

"Why not?"

"It's a matter of principle. I don't read your letters—why should you read mine?"

"I'm interested in everything you do."

"All right. If you must know, they've narrowed their list down to three candidates. They'd like me to fly out for an interview."

"When?"

"Anytime in the next month."

"Well, that's good news, isn't it?"

"I don't know if it is or not."

"Let's say you got the job. Would you want me to move there with you?"

"The question is, would you want to quit your job and school here?"

"I want to be with you wherever you are."

He looked at her as if he were doing a calculation in his head. She knew he was counting up the advantages and disadvantages of taking her along if he moved to California. She knew him well enough by now to know he never did anything on pure emotion. His mind always controlled his heart. That's why he was so successful in his job.

He finished eating and left to go take a shower.

She sat and tried to think about what she should do to keep Ryan. She would quit her job and withdraw from school immediately and move to California with him if he asked her to, but she wasn't sure he would ask her. He hated to admit he couldn't get along without someone.

A week later Ryan's car wouldn't start, so she drove him to work. When they pulled up in front of the office building where he worked, there was a car in front of them. A woman was taking her husband to work. Before he got out of the car, the man leaned over and kissed his wife.

"Are you going to kiss me like that when you get out of the car?" Debra asked, halfway joking.

"You know that's not my style."

"Why isn't it?"

"Because I'm not a sloppy, sentimental Mormon."

"You don't have to be a Mormon to kiss someone goodbye on your way to work."

"You knew what I was like before you moved in with me. If that's not good enough for you, just say the word."

"Here we are, sir, at your destination."

He opened the door. "I'll see you tonight."

"Ryan, I really do love you. You know that, don't you?"

"Not now, Debra. I'm nearly late for work now as it is." He shut the door and walked away and never looked back.

It wasn't a surprise. She thought about the time she had hinted her birthday was coming up and he handed her some money and told her to get something for herself. She'd said it would mean more to her if he picked something out himself, and he said, "I don't have time for that."

"Then you're too busy."

"You knew what I was like when you moved in."

"Are you trying to get rid of me?"

"No, I just want you to stop trying to change me."

Early on Thursday, March 15, Ryan flew to Sacramento, California, for a job interview. He flew back that evening, and she picked him up at the airport. As they headed home, he offered no news about the trip.

She wasn't sure why she'd done it, but she'd spent the afternoon making spaghetti for him, just the way he liked it.

After dessert, he asked for another cup of coffee.

"Are you going to tell me what happened?" she asked.

"They offered me the job."

"Did you accept their offer?"

"Tentatively."

"So you're moving to California?"

"Not necessarily. I told them I wouldn't take the job unless I got a fifteen percent raise over what they were paying the person before me, so that's still up in the air. There're still a few things that could stop it from going through."

"Ryan, I can't walk away from everything at a moment's notice. When does your job start in California?"

"Well, actually, as soon as I can get there. We've discussed having me start in a couple of weeks."

Her mouth dropped. Looking at him, she already knew what he had decided. "You don't want me to go with you, do you." It was a statement, not a question.

"We need to be reasonable about this, Debra. I'll be ten times busier there than I ever was here. I'm not sure you'd ever see me. Besides, Utah is your home. You probably wouldn't even like Sacramento."

"Shouldn't that be up to me to decide?"

He sighed. "You're not making this easy for me, you know."

"I know you've rehearsed your little speech in the plane, so just go ahead and give it."

"This is a new phase in my life, and I want to start off with no baggage from the past. I've enjoyed the time we've spent together, but, let's face it, it's time for us both to move on."

"You're the one that's moving on, not me."

"Oh, good grief, c'mon, Debra. You're not going to play the desperate woman, are you? Don't. It doesn't work with me, so don't embarrass yourself by falling to pieces, and whatever you do, don't start crying. I can't stand that."

"Just answer me this—in what way was I inadequate?"

"I told you already that I enjoyed our time together. What do you want, a letter of recommendation?"

He was right, it would do no good to argue with him. Once he made up his mind, he never budged.

She stood up. "Excuse me. I need to pack up my things."

"You're welcome to stay until the end of the month. You've paid for it anyway, and it'd give you a chance to find yourself another place. I suppose you could just stay here after I leave, but of course it almost takes two people to be able to afford the place."

"I wouldn't think of staying here." She stood up. "I'll take a few of my things now and come back for the rest later."

It took her five minutes to pack a suitcase. Ryan, wanting to avoid a scene, left in his car and said he'd be back in an hour.

That's all there is to it, she thought as she pulled out of the driveway.

There was no place for her to go — not anymore. She drove south on the interstate until she got tired and found a cheap motel and spent the night there.

The next day, Friday, she skipped classes and called in sick at work. At eleven that morning she returned to the apartment. Ryan's car was gone. She parked in front of the apartment and went inside. She felt like a stranger going into someone else's home.

On the telephone stand she saw Ryan's list of what he needed to do in preparation for moving to California. She glanced down at the list. At first she expected to find "Break up with Debra" listed and dutifully checked off, but it wasn't there. There was no mention of her. It was as if she had never existed in his life.

She decided he must have made up the list last night after she'd left. Since he'd taken care of her, there was no need to put her on it. He hadn't wasted any time feeling bad about their breaking up. That was so much like Ryan.

It was odd. One of the things that first attracted her to him, that he was such a goal-directed person, was the very thing that allowed him to terminate their relationship when he no longer needed her. She wondered if he had someone already lined up in California. That would be like him. He always had a plan to get what he wanted.

She walked into the bedroom. Several boxes were on the floor. She looked in a couple of them. They were filled with her things, carefully folded and neatly arranged in the boxes. At first she was angry at him for touching her clothes. Realistically, though, she knew he probably felt he had no choice. He had to be out of the apartment by the end of the month, and he had no way of knowing when she would come back to get her things.

She carried each box out to the car, filling up the trunk first and then putting what was left in the back seat of her car. *So much for the bedroom,* she thought.

She took one last look around the place before leaving. They had experienced good times, but she knew that she wouldn't think back on them much because of the way this was ending. She had been in love, but now she knew he'd never felt the same way about her. She wasn't sure if he was even capable of real love.

She found an empty box in the living room and used it to pack up her things in the bathroom. He had taken all the towels except one, so the room had a hollow echo now that hadn't been there before. She nearly forgot her robe hanging on a hook on the back of the bathroom door. His robe was hanging there too. It still had his smell on it. There had been times, when he was out of town on a trip and she was all alone in the apartment, when she'd worn it because it reminded her of him. Today she didn't even touch it.

On the kitchen table she found an empty pizza box, two plates, and two glasses. Whoever had used the extra plate had not eaten the outer crust of two pieces. She picked up the glass. She could detect a trace of lipstick on it.

Now she knew why her clothes had been packed so neatly. Ryan must have asked Sharla, his secretary, to come and help him. That was so much like Ryan. Once he was finished with something, he was finished totally. *He didn't even want to touch anything of mine again,* she thought.

She rummaged through the kitchen drawers and took out the pots and pans she had brought with her when she had moved in with Ryan. She got an empty box from the bedroom and packed up the kitchen items. After she carried the box out to the car, she took one last pass through the apartment.

She picked up his list again and studied it. Suddenly she realized that he was planning to leave next Monday. That meant he had given two weeks' notice to the landlord before he'd even left for California. The apartment manager had known before she had. She knew the reason he didn't tell her until the very last was so he wouldn't be alone until he was ready to leave town. *I really pick 'em,* she said to herself.

She paused at the door. *Is this all there is to it? You just pack up your things and walk away, and nobody cares how you feel because you were only living together anyway.*

She got in the car and then realized she still had her key to the apartment. If she kept it, she knew Ryan would phone and ask her to return it so they could get their deposit back. She didn't want to talk to him ever again, so she went back inside and put the key on the kitchen table.

She ripped off a piece of paper from the notepad Ryan had been using to make his list and took a pen from her purse. She tried to think what she should say. *What do you say when you've given all the love you have to offer, but it wasn't enough to make it last?* she thought. No, there was nothing she wanted to say, so she just wrote, "Here's my key. Please send my share of the deposit to me at work." She didn't even sign her name. *He'll be able to figure out who it is. At least in the next couple of days he will,* she thought, *but in ten years he'll have even forgotten my name.*

She drove to a shopping mall and parked the car. Then she sat in the car and watched the people come and go.

A young mother parked beside her. Two kids were in car seats in the back. She opened the door and unbuckled them. She put the younger child in a stroller, and the older child toddled along behind her.

She's LDS, Debra thought. There had been a time when

she would have scorned the woman because of being around Ryan, who had always enjoyed ridiculing Mormon women.

The woman looked to be close to her age. Debra thought about going up and talking to her. It would be nice to know about her children. They looked adorable, and the woman seemed happy.

I'm not going to cry, she told herself. *Crying would be wrong because it would mean that Ryan has won. Why should I cry? Ryan will never cry for me. He'll just find someone to take my place. Ryan never looks back. That's why he's such a great success in life.*

An elderly couple walked past her. The man seemed confused about where the car was parked but his wife knew. "It's in the next row," she said.

"Are you sure?" he asked.

"It's at D-7," she said.

The man smiled. "What would I ever do without you?"

"You'd have to wait until the mall closed before you could find where you parked, dear."

"That's for sure."

They got in their car and the woman drove. Debra imagined that for much of their married life he had driven but that because of failing eyesight or for some other reason, he had had to give up and let her drive. *For all these years,* she thought, *she's probably been better at driving but she's kept it to herself because it wasn't important.* Maybe it was like that with her own parents. She remembered a trip they took to Disneyland when her father had driven the entire way. Whenever her mother asked if he wanted her to drive, he always said, "I'm not tired."

It had been a long time since she'd talked to them on the phone. Her mother always asked her to come visit them and to bring Ryan with her, but her father never did. She had been avoiding her parents ever since she moved in with Ryan.

A carload of girls pulled into a nearby space. They were

105

chattering about boys, about clothes, about everything girls talk about when they go to a mall.

One of the girls stopped to look in the mirror of a parked car. "I hate my hair," she said.

"It's okay."

"No, it's ugly."

"No, really, it's fine."

Debra could see herself and Michelle in those two girls, the way they'd been. They looked happy. *I was happy once, but that was a long time ago,* she thought. Just then a moan escaped her lips. It was loud enough that one of the girls turned back to see where the sound had come from, but, seeing nothing, she headed into the mall with her friends.

Debra sobbed. "I've got to talk to Michelle right away," she whispered to herself.

10

"This is Debra. Is there any way I can reach Michelle now? It's kind of important."

"Let's see, she doesn't have any classes today, so I think she's working. Let me give you her work number. I know she'd like to see you." Michelle's mother gave her the number, then said, "Debra, have you talked to your parents lately?"

"Not lately."

"I think you should. They're really worried about you."

"I'll go see them real soon," she said.

She reached Michelle at the BYU Bookstore and arranged to meet her for lunch at the Wilkinson Center the next day.

She waited until they got their food and found a table before she unloaded her problems. "Ryan's got a new job. He's moving to California."

"Are you going with him?"

"No. He doesn't want me to. Ryan likes to keep all his options open."

"I'm sorry."

"Hey, that's the way it goes. I'll be all right. Somebody else will come along sometime." She paused. "You think I'm stupid, don't you, to keep getting involved with men I'm not married to. Well, that's the way it is these days. People have other opinions about this than what you've been taught. There's no such a thing as lasting happiness. You wait, Michelle—one of these days you'll see that Shane isn't your knight in shining armor. He's got faults like everybody else. It won't matter if you've been married in the temple or not. That's just the way it is."

"I know there'll be problems in our marriage; there is in every marriage. But we've made a commitment to work out whatever problems come along. One thing's for certain, he's not going to walk out on me just because he gets a job in another town." There was a brief, painful silence. "I'm sorry. I shouldn't have said that."

Debra tried to smile. "Why don't we argue about something easy, like politics?"

"Have you talked to your parents lately?"

"No."

"I think you should."

"Everyone thinks I should talk to my parents."

"Why don't you then?"

"I guess maybe because it's so painful to try and find something safe we can talk about."

It was almost time for Michelle to go back to work. "You want some free advice?"

"Hey, why not? I can use all the help I can get."

"I think you should talk to the bishop in our home ward."

"What for?"

"He might be able to help you. What if God is trying to get a message to you?"

"I think he should just fax it."

"Are you going to stand in the reception line with me on my wedding day?"

"No."

"Why not?"

"I don't feel welcome at the church anymore."

"That's why you should talk to the bishop. At least one time. What harm can it do?"

*   *   *

108

"How can I help you?" the bishop asked.

"To tell you the truth, I'm not really sure you can," Debra said. "Coming here was Michelle's idea. I don't even go to church anymore. I used to, though, a long time ago. But then something happened." She paused. "I've been disfellow-shipped."

"Do you want to come back to the Church?"

"Not really. Actually all I want to do is to stand in the reception line at Michelle's wedding. She asked me, you know. We were best friends in school."

"You don't have to be active in the Church to stand in a reception line."

"Oh, I know that. It's just that I'd be seeing all the people I knew in church when I was growing up — the teachers I had in Primary and Young Women — and them knowing all about what happened to me. I'm not sure I want to be reminded how far I've gone astray from the way I was taught."

"I still don't understand why you've come to see me. You don't need my permission to stand in Michelle's reception line."

"Well, actually there is another reason. Things haven't been going real well in my life . . . Boy, is that an understatement! The guy I was living with broke up with me because he got himself another job in California and he didn't want me tagging along. I really loved him too, so that was a major disappoint-ment. Also, I haven't been real close to my mom and dad, and now I'm starting to think that maybe I should try and patch things up between us. And then I've met the guy Michelle's going to marry. They both look so happy. You know that story about the man who sold his birthright for some pottage, what-ever that is. Well, I've been thinking: What if that's what I've done? I hope you don't mind me rambling on like this. I'm usually very well organized . . . Do you have a tissue? Thanks . . . Okay, the thing is, I don't know what to do next. What would I have to do to get completely back into the Church? I don't mean as far as the red tape goes — but as far as changing my life."

"You'd have to go through the process of repentance."

"Okay, you mean like going to church, and not smoking or drinking or using coffee, right? To tell you the truth, I'm not sure I want to be a member of the Church. There's too many things you have to do when you're a member. Can I tell you what the Church is like for somebody like me?"

"Please do."

"I've read a lot of self-help books. You wouldn't believe all the books I've read — books on improving your vocabulary, books on not letting people push you around, books on what colors of clothes you should wear, books on makeup and grooming and dressing for success, books on improving your voice and how to walk so you inspire confidence, books on being a good conversationalist — hundreds of books. Well, okay, every book ends up with a few things you should always do, like when I walk, I should keep my stomach in, and for speaking I should keep my soft palate up — you know, so I don't come out with a little girl voice — and when I walk I should keep my shoulders back so I'm not all slumped over. The thing is, after you've read fifty or so of these books, and each one has two or three things you should always do, pretty soon there's so many things to think about. I remember this one time I was at a party and a stranger walked up to me and I was so busy worrying about whether my stomach was in and my shoulders back and my soft palate up that I couldn't concentrate on what I should say. I got over that eventually, but to me that's what it's like to be a member of the Church. You've got food storage and genealogy and chastity and not drinking and not thinking bad thoughts — it's just too much. Everyone trying to be perfect but nobody succeeding. Who needs it? That's what I want to know."

"There's only one thing you need to work on in this church, and that is to remember the Savior and keep his command-

110

ments." He found a scripture in Moroni in the Book of Mormon and handed it to Debra. "Read verses 32 through 34 please."

" 'Yea, come unto Christ, and be perfected in him, and deny yourselves of all ungodliness; and if ye shall deny yourselves of all ungodliness, and love God with all your might, mind and strength, then is his grace sufficient for you, that by his grace ye may be perfect in Christ; and if by the grace of God ye are perfect in Christ, ye can in nowise deny the power of God. And again, if ye by the grace of God are perfect in Christ, and deny not his power, then are ye sanctified in Christ by the grace of God, through the shedding of the blood of Christ, which is in the covenant of the Father unto the remission of your sins, that ye become holy, without spot.' "

"We don't perfect ourselves by going through a never-ending checklist," the bishop said. "It comes through the grace of Christ."

She looked again at what she'd read. "This part about becoming holy, without spot—can that happen to someone like me who's made a lot of mistakes?"

"Yes."

"What would I have to do?"

"You'd have to put your trust in the Savior and give away all your sins."

"Maybe you should know what I've done wrong... I've been sleeping around, off and on, since I was fifteen. I can't even remember some of their names. It's no good, I know that now. With any guy, no matter how great we got along at first, I always knew it would end someday. It's just a matter of time. And there's always the worry about getting pregnant or getting a sexually transmitted disease. So I've learned there's a lot of really good reasons to live the way the Church teaches. If you'd ever want me to talk to some of your youth, I could tell them what I've learned."

"The only thing anyone needs to know is that chastity is a commandment of God. Do you understand how much you've

111

offended God by the way you've been living? Debra, come back to the Savior and his teachings and his church."

The phone rang. He picked it up. " . . . Yes, I'll be right there."

He hung up.

"I'm keeping you from something, aren't I?"

"Yes, but I want to continue our discussion later on. Will you come back?"

"I don't want to waste your time."

"This isn't a waste of my time. Would you mind if I gave you some homework?"

"Like what?"

"I'd like you to begin reading the Book of Mormon every day. And I'd like you to underline every passage that refers to the mission of Jesus Christ. I want you also to be prepared to tell me if you understand the seriousness of your transgressions. On Sunday I'd like you here in church on the front row so I can see you. I want you to be prepared to tell me in detail the events in the Garden of Gethsemane and also the events leading up to and including the crucifixion. I want you to understand that the Savior can help you turn your life around. You can't do it on your own—you have to rely on him for your salvation. You can be forgiven and start over."

"That's a lot of homework, isn't it?"

"I'm here to help you get to a point where the Savior can perform the miracle of forgiveness in your life. Will you come back to see me?"

She thought about it. "To tell you the truth, I'm not that sure I want to go through with this."

"It's up to you. One other thing."

"What?"

"Go visit your mom and dad."

*　　　　*　　　　*

The next morning Debra woke up in her old bedroom. She'd moved back home the night before. She would never forget what it had been like when her parents came to the door and saw her standing there with Michelle. They hugged and cried and there were no accusations between them.

And now she was home. She wasn't sure how it was going to work out. Most likely she'd move again in a few weeks, but this would give her a start in making changes in her life.

As she looked around the room, it was like going back in time. A yellowed newspaper clipping of when she was a cheerleader for ninth grade basketball . . . a plastic trophy inscribed with "World's Greatest Bowler" some boy had given her after taking her bowling in the summer before she started high school . . . snapshots of her and Michelle . . . a stack of English papers she'd saved because the teacher had written something complimentary about what she'd written . . . a closet full of clothes that should have been taken long ago to the Deseret Industries.

It was only six in the morning, but it was the only time she could complete the bishop's reading assignment.

There was a knock on the door. It was her father. "Breakfast is ready."

She went into the kitchen. She knew, of course, what they would be having for breakfast — the only thing her father liked: hot oatmeal, toast, and orange juice. Some things you can count on, she thought as she sat down to the table with her parents. Her mother said the blessing.

At first they ate without talking. Then she asked, "Mom and Dad, do you think it's even worth trying to change my life around?"

"Oh, yes, it's worth it!" her mother said, suddenly hopeful again that things would change.

"Dad, what do you think?"

He put down his spoon. "When we first moved into this

house, the paint on the outside was peeling. I had a painter come out and look at it. He said that whoever had built the house hadn't put on primer first before painting it. He said the only thing I could do was to scrape down to the bare wood, prime it, and then repaint over that. It seemed like too much work but he said that if we didn't do that, if we just painted it again, then in a few years the new paint would start cracking too. So that's what we did, sanded down to the bare wood, and then did what should have been done from the beginning. You can see for yourself that it worked. I think that's what you have to do on yourself. It'll take some work, but when you're through, you'll feel good about what you've done. I've always known that deep down you were a good girl."

"You can do it, Debra," her mother said. "I know you can."

"What if I don't? Can you love me even if I'm not living the way you want me to?"

"We never stopped loving you. And we never will."

"That's good. I love you both too. I'm sorry for what I've put you through."

There was a long pause and then her mother dabbed at her eyes with her napkin and said, "You're back now, that's the important thing."

"You'd better eat your oatmeal before it gets cold," her father said.

While she was eating, something remarkable happened. It was like seeing her parents for the very first time, seeing them on an adult-to-adult basis. All the time she was growing up, she didn't really notice much about them. Her mother was the disapproving glance when she came out of her bedroom wearing some bizarre outfit; her father was the stern voice that tried to turn her away from the path she'd chosen to follow. In a way, during those years, someone could have replaced her parents with cardboard cutouts and she wouldn't have noticed. Sometimes, even, she had been embarrassed that her parents weren't as outwardly impressive as some others. But now she felt as though she were seeing them for the first time. All during breakfast there was a calmness about them as they talked about what they were going to do that day. She noticed how much of their time and thoughts was spent in trying to help others.

"I think you're both so wonderful," she said as she took her bowl and spoon to the sink.

"Oh, not us, we're just ordinary."

"Mom, Dad, look — no matter what happens, I want to thank you for raising me. You taught me the right way. All the mistakes I've made, I've made on my own. I just wanted you to know that."

Her mother began to cry. Her father sat stone-faced but dabbing at his eyes with a napkin.

She hugged them both and then it was too much and her tears came and she had to leave the room.

11

Summer 1990

Over the summer Debra's life began to fall into a safe and comfortable pattern. She lived with her parents and went to school and worked. She met once a week with the bishop and gradually began to feel more comfortable in church again. She also began to attend single adult activities. They helped fill the void, but she kept thinking there must be more to life than cookies and punch laced with Seven-Up.

One great benefit of her having moved back in with her parents is that for the first time since she could remember, they now were able to talk about things they had never been able to talk about before. She also told Michelle that she would stand with her in the receiving line at her reception, and so she and her mother worked together to make her bridesmaid's dress.

She didn't hear anything from Ryan, but that didn't really surprise her.

August 1990

Michelle's wedding was scheduled for Friday morning, August 24, in the Salt Lake Temple. On Monday morning Debra received a phone call from Ryan. "I'd like you to move out here."

"Why?"

"I miss you. You can continue going to college here and I've found you a job like what you're doing there but it pays almost twice as much, so it'd be worth it for you to move."

"You haven't said the magic words yet."

"Don't make me beg, Debra. You know that's not my style."

"Do you love me, Ryan?"

"I think I probably do. You know that's not easy for me to say."

"I know it isn't. Let's say I did move out there. Any chance we could get married before I moved in with you?"

He cleared his throat. "I've come a long ways but I haven't come that far. But now at least I'm willing to discuss it."

"There's something you should know. I've started to go back to church."

"I thought you'd outgrown all that. Look, I've booked you for a flight here on Friday. You can pick your ticket up at the airport in Salt Lake. Just pack up and come out here."

"Friday's not such a good time. My friend Michelle has asked me to stand in her reception line on Friday night."

"She'll understand if you can't make it. Besides, I want you here so we can get settled over the weekend."

"I'll need time to think about it."

"All right. Call me tomorrow and let me know what you've decided. Debra, if you come here, it'll be just the way it used to be."

"So, that's it," Debra said after Michelle got home from work Monday afternoon. "On Friday I make either you or Ryan happy."

Michelle suddenly stood up. "Look, don't go away. I'll be back in half an hour."

When Michelle returned, she had a silly smile on her face. She jingled a set of keys. "Guess what these are?"

117

"They're keys, right?"

"Right, but keys to what?"

"I give up."

"Keys to girls' camp. Nobody's up there tonight. I got permission and everything. Let's go camp out, just the two of us."

"I'm sure Shane doesn't want you running off just before you get married."

"He's going out with a friend of his from high school tonight. C'mon, what do you say? It'll be fun. It's my last chance to be a girl before I get married."

By the time they'd cooked their hobo dinners in the glowing embers and cleaned up, it was dark. They sat around the fire and roasted marshmallows.

"I think you should meet Shane's friend Matt from Montana. He's really something else. And he says he wants to settle down and get married."

"No, thanks. My life is complicated enough as it is."

They walked down to the lake and sat on the dock and watched the moon come up. "Just like old times, right?" Michelle said.

"No, not really, but at least you're more like you were then than I am."

"Why did things turn out so different for us?"

"I thought I could live on the edge and not fall off. It doesn't work that way."

"Have you decided yet about moving in with Ryan?"

"It could work out, you know, if I went back to him. We could get married eventually, and then maybe sometime he'd join the Church, and then I'd have what you're going to have."

"Has he ever shown any interest in the Church?"

"No."

"What if he's never ready to get married? Can you be happy not having the Church in your life?"

"It's like I either have to give up the Church or Ryan. That's not an easy choice, you know."

"Ryan's not the only guy in the world. There are others, you know, even members of the Church."

"Not like Ryan."

"That's right, not like Ryan. Some guys around here are much better."

"So where are you hiding them? Look, let's talk about you for a while—the girl who made her dreams come true. That is you, isn't it?"

"Yes, I guess it is."

"Seeing you now makes me wish I'd waited. I've used sex as a toy, but you've held back so you can show Shane how much you love him. I think he's a very lucky guy."

"We're both lucky. Debra, you can still come back to the Church. Why don't you?"

"It's not easy to admit I've been wrong most of my life. The way I carried on when I was in high school didn't bring me any happiness. I know that now. Too bad I didn't know it then."

"There's a woman I work with in the bookstore at BYU. She's got a daughter named Kristen who's giving her a rough time. She's doing some of the same kinds of things you did. Do you suppose you could write her a letter? Maybe if you wrote her and told her what you've learned, it would help her. You wouldn't have to sign your name or anything. She might listen to you."

"I'll think about it." She looked at her watch. "We'd better get some sleep. I don't want Shane mad at me on your wedding night because you caught a cold tonight."

After getting ready for bed, they had a prayer and then lay down in their sleeping bags.

A minute later there was a loud crunching sound in the tent.

"What was that?" Debra asked.

119

Michelle sat up and thrust a box at Debra. "Gingersnaps. I brought you gingersnaps!"

The next day Debra had an appointment scheduled with the bishop. She wasn't going to keep it but Michelle talked her into it. The first thing she said after the bishop closed his door was, "Ryan's asked me to come back and live with him."

"That would be a big mistake."

"Why would it?"

"Because it's wrong."

"Why is it wrong?"

"It's against God's commandments."

"Are there any other reasons besides that?"

"None of the other reasons are as important."

"Why can't you people be more reasonable?"

"God isn't liberal about the law of chastity. If you go and live with Ryan, it won't bring you lasting happiness."

"How can you know that?"

"Because wickedness was never happiness."

"Why should I go back to a church that makes me feel bad? I don't need this. I don't need people looking down their noses at me. I don't need any of it. Look, after my first time with a guy, I went back to church and tried to live the way I should but it didn't make any difference. I did everything I was supposed to but it still didn't go any good. I still felt guilty, like I didn't belong there. So don't ask me to go through that again. I don't like feeling bad about myself."

"Just quitting a sin doesn't mean you've repented."

"I went to church, I went to seminary, I did all the things I was supposed to do, but none of it made any difference."

"Did you go to your bishop and tell him what had happened?"

"No."

"You should have."

"Why?"

120

"So he could have helped you in the repentance process."

"What could he have done? I was already doing all the things I was supposed to do."

The bishop, in deep thought, stopped talking and lowered his gaze. For a long time he didn't say anything. Debra wondered if his silence meant she'd won the debate. When he finally looked up, she noticed tears in his eyes. In a voice so soft she had to lean forward to hear it, he said, "Debra, remember this one thing. You have to depend on the Savior to be cleansed and forgiven of your sins. He's the only one who can make you feel whole again . . . the only one . . . he is the only one."

He turned to a passage in the Book of Mormon. "Here, in the twenty-fifth chapter of Second Nephi, will you read verse 23?"

She took the book and read: " 'For we labor diligently to write, to persuade our children, and also our brethren, to believe in Christ, and to be reconciled to God; for we know that it is by grace that we are saved, after all we can do.' "

"None of us will ever be saved without Jesus Christ," the bishop said. "We have to try as hard as we can, and then leave the rest to him. That's why we ask people to go to their bishop, because he understands the process of repentance. Forgiveness of your past is here for you if you sincerely want it."

She thought about it for a long time. "That's just it. I'm not sure I want it that bad."

"What's standing in your way?"

"I'm in love." She stood up. "Thanks for helping me make up my mind. I've just decided to go to California on Friday. Michelle doesn't really need me to stand in her reception line. I've got my own life to worry about. Thanks for trying to help me."

"I wish you well."

"Thank you for your time."

She went home, phoned Ryan and told him she was coming, and started packing.

12

August 24, 1990

At five thirty Friday morning, Debra heard two cars pull up next door. She looked out her window. Shane and his family had come to have breakfast before heading for the Salt Lake Temple.

At six fifteen a procession of people began carrying things out to the car — the wedding dress, temple clothes in suitcases — family members getting into their cars to go to the temple.

Debra watched them leave. She realized it was probably the last time she'd see Michelle. Once she got to California, she didn't plan on ever coming back.

Her parents had not taken her decision to go back to Ryan very well. She knew how disappointed in her they were.

This is a big day for Michelle and for me too, she thought. *A new beginning for both of us.*

Her plane didn't leave until noon. She had decided she would take a taxi — she didn't want to have her mother crying as she boarded the plane. It was much better to get all that taken care of at home. She was packed except for a scrapbook her mother had given her last night. It had all the pictures they'd ever taken of her, all the certificates and awards from school, even report cards from first grade.

Because she had time to kill and she wasn't sleepy anymore, she sat in bed and thumbed through the scrapbook. She saw herself at age nine standing with her parents in front of Old Faithful geyser in Yellowstone National Park. She'd forgotten about family vacations.

On the next page was a picture of herself and her father, taken at a PTA fund-raising carnival. She was proudly holding a cake. She remembered winning the "cake walk." The reason her dad was in the picture was because he'd been asked to be in charge of the carnival that year. She'd forgotten about PTA.

On the next page she saw herself in Primary, standing with her father at a daddy-daughter party. She'd forgotten about daddy-daughter parties.

There were pictures of her and Michelle, including some taken at girls' camp. She'd forgotten all about many of those activities.

There were pictures of her and Michelle's sister, Andrea. Andrea was married now and had two children. She lived in Idaho Falls.

By the time she realized what looking at the scrapbook had done to her, it was too late. The damage was done. She had questions she needed Ryan to answer. She looked at the clock. It was seven thirty. Michelle would be in the temple now. In California it was only six thirty. Ryan still had fifteen more minutes to sleep. He always got up at six forty-five. She reached for the phone and dialed his number. "Yes," he said in his usual no-nonsense version of hello.

"Ryan, there's some questions I need you to answer. First of all, someday I'll want to have children. What would you think about that?"

"You're not pregnant now, though, are you?"

"No."

"So you're talking about something in the future then, right?"

"Yes."

"Well, I suppose that's a possibility. We'd have to talk about it and make sure that's what we both want."

"If we did have children, I'd want for us to be married, wouldn't you?"

"Well, yes, I guess so."

"And I'd want our kids to go to church with me."

"They'd be Mormons?"

"Yes."

"If you have to have a religion, I suppose it's as good as any."

"And when they're in grade school, the school might want you to serve in PTA. Have I ever told you my dad was in charge of a PTA carnival in my school when I was in fifth grade? You'd be good at that too, if you'd agree to do it. Or maybe they'd ask you to coach a Little League team. And when our kids get sick, I'd want you to give them a priesthood blessing. But before you did that, you'd have to join the Church."

"Is all of this absolutely necessary?"

"It's what I had, Ryan, when I was growing up. I want it for my kids too." She paused. "There's more, too. I'd want you to kiss me when you leave for work in the morning and kiss me when you come back each night. I'd want us to have prayers together as a family. I want us to go on family vacations in a big station wagon — and maybe even have a dog, although the dog is optional."

There was a long pause. "Debra, if you're really serious about all this, maybe you've got the wrong man."

It took forever to say it. "Maybe I have."

"We almost made it though, didn't we?"

"Almost, Ryan, almost. I'll send you back the ticket."

By the time she got dressed and drove to Temple Square, it was ten fifteen. Her father, who worked in the temple once a week, had told her he didn't expect Michelle and Shane would be out until after eleven, so she had time. She sat down and waited. She knew that they would come out and have their

124

pictures taken on the steps of the temple, so that's where she'd meet them.

While she waited, she decided to see what she could write for the girl Michelle told her about. She took out a small notebook and a pen and began writing. After half an hour she read what she'd written:

"Dear Kristen,

"Don't make the same mistakes I made. I lived a wild life and after all that, this is what I found out:

"If you use sex just for fun, you'll end up getting used.

"If you have sex with just anyone who comes along, after a while nobody worthwhile comes along.

"If you have sex just because it feels good, you'll end up feeling bad.

"Going to bed with someone to prove you love him is like trying to prove how healthy your heart is by cutting it out and passing it around for everyone to take a look.

"Having sex to satisfy your curiosity takes away your sense of wonder.

"Now I know that sexual freedom isn't free. There's a big price that has to be paid. For one thing, the way I was living made me feel bad about myself. Also, I pulled away from God because I knew what I was doing was wrong. It's kind of scary to feel like you can't count on God's help anymore because of the way you're living, because when things go wrong you feel like you're totally on your own. Another price I had to pay was waking up every day knowing how much I'd disappointed my mom and dad. I couldn't see it then, but now I know that all they ever wanted was for me to be happy. I wished I'd listened to them more than I did.

"I hope you'll believe me when I tell you that the best way to live is the way your parents say. Listen to them and don't make the same mistakes I've made.

Love,

Debra, your secret friend"

She had a few minutes so she went to the Visitors' Center and walked up the ramp to the statue of the *Christus*. She sat there for several minutes and thought about how, this time, she would put her trust in Jesus and let him cleanse her and heal her and make her clean again. She realized now she couldn't do it on her own.

She wanted to get a message to Jesus but she didn't know how. Then she decided to pray to God and ask him to give a message to his Son. *Jesus, I've messed up my life and made a lot of mistakes and disappointed you and Heavenly Father and my parents and the people I grew up with in the Church, but now I want to start all over again and live the way I should. From now on I'll try to do what you want me to do and never repeat the mistakes I've made in the past. I want to start all over again, like I tried to do before, but this time I'll lean on you and not try to do it by myself. Oh, dear Jesus, please help me. Please forgive me and take away my guilt and do all the things I can't do for myself.*

And then the tears came and she let them, even though people were walking past her. A feeling came over her and she knew that she would not be left alone to make the changes she had to make in her life.

Before she left, she pulled out her notebook and added a postscript to her note to Kristen.

"P.S. I've given you some reasons I learned why it's better to live the way the Church teaches. But there's something else I've just found out, not from the life I lived, but from the things I've read in the scriptures and from the bishop who's trying to help me change. Above anything else, please remember that the number one reason for living the law of chastity is because it's a commandment from God. God and Jesus love us and want us to be happy, but they know we can't be happy if we're breaking the law of chastity.

"I hope my letter helps you some.

Love, Debra"

126

A little past eleven thirty the wedding party came to the steps of the temple for pictures. Debra stood off to the side as the photographer began taking pictures of the bride and groom. At first nobody noticed her, and then Michelle's mother turned and saw her and called out, "Michelle, Debra's here!"

"Where?" And then Michelle saw her. She hurried down the stairs as best she could in her wedding dress and threw her arms around her. "You're here! You're here! Oh, I'm so glad you're here!"

"You're going to mess up your face with those tears," Debra said.

"Hey, it's worth it."

"Look, Michelle, I'm yours for the day. If you need me to help decorate the cultural hall or run errands or anything else—I've got nothing else to do all day. I'm not going to California. I'm staying here."

"This is the happiest day of my life and you've made it even more wonderful. You'll stand in the reception line now, won't you?"

"If you still want me."

"Of course I do." Michelle then spoke confidentially so nobody else could overhear. "You've got to meet Shane's friend Matt from Montana. Guess what? He's been asking some questions about the Church. Isn't that promising?"

The photographer was getting impatient to finish up, and there was another wedding party anxious to get their pictures taken too. Shane came down the steps to where Debra and Michelle were standing.

"Hey, remember me?" he said with a smile.

"Aren't you the guy I just got married to?"

"Yep, that's me."

"Well . . . aren't I the lucky one!"

They went back up for more pictures. Debra was standing there, glowing in the happiness of her best friend, when she sensed someone had come up next to her.

"I understand we'll be stringing crepe paper together to-day," a deep voice said, "so I thought we should get better acquainted."

She turned and saw a younger version of Tom Selleck standing there.

"I'm Shane's friend from Montana."

Her eyes opened wide. "You're Matt?"

13

August 24, 1990: Michelle and Shane

Shane could hear Michelle brushing her teeth in the bathroom. He thought back to what it had been like in the temple as they knelt at the altar and held hands across it. He thought about Michelle's smile and how beautiful she looked — and how much better he felt when he was with her. He thought about being surrounded by their families, and the peace and serenity he'd felt. *Serenity,* he thought. *That's another word that begins with S.* Ever since he'd given her the paper-clip necklace, they'd both searched for the perfect word that began with S. *Serenity describes Michelle,* he thought.

A thousand thoughts raced through his mind. This was the day he'd been dreaming about for so long and now it was here. He'd made it.

There were times when he was growing up that his wedding day seemed a million miles away. When he was fourteen or fifteen it was hard to imagine that his wedding day would be enriched or impoverished by what he did or didn't do then. And yet, looking back now he could see that every day had been important in determining what this day would be like for him. It wasn't just the obvious things, like keeping himself morally clean, that had made this day possible. It was that he'd had enough experiences with finding out that he was a person of worth, not just because of what he had done, but because of who he was. He liked himself and he knew that was important, because if he didn't think he could succeed, nobody else would believe it either.

Now his time of waiting was over. It was time to celebrate life and love and devotion to one another.

At that moment Michelle too felt at peace with herself. This had been the happiest day of her life. Being married in the temple had been everything she had hoped it would be—a rich spiritual experience, a family reunion, a party with all her favorite people in attendance, a victory celebration. It was like a prayer being given and answered at the same time. There were blessings of eternity promised as well as blessings to be realized that very day.

It had happened. After all this time it had finally happened.

Michelle took a deep breath, opened the door, and stepped out. Shane stood up.

"Hello there, Mister Husband," she said softly.

"You look . . . real . . . good," he said, in what he realized was the understatement of the century.

"Thank you."

He noticed she was wearing her paper-clip necklace. "I know what the S stands for tonight," he said.

"What?"

"It stands for Celebration."

She smiled. "Celebration is a wonderful S word."

"Tonight it is." He took her in his arms and kissed her.

August 25, 1990

When Shane woke up the next morning, for a brief instant he didn't know what time it was or even what day it was. He looked at the clock next to the bed. It was nine fifteen. Many people were already up and moving about, and here he was just waking up for the first time with Michelle. She was still

130

asleep. He couldn't get over how beautiful she was, her noble chin, her dark eyebrows, her tawny skin, her soft and inviting lips. *My wife,* he thought, smiling to himself. *My wonderful, beautiful, talented, smart wife. How did I ever get so lucky?*

He sat up in bed. Sunlight was coming in through breaks in the curtains. He got out of bed and opened the curtains and looked out at the city below, filled with cars driven by people in a hurry to get somewhere. He didn't want to go anywhere; he was happy just where he was.

The sunshine streaming in the room woke Michelle, and she sat up. He went over to the bed and put his arms around her and kissed her. "I've been watching you sleep," he said. "You're absolutely the most beautiful woman in the world."

"How nice to wake up with a compliment. I want to be beautiful for you."

He put his arm around her. "You are. Yesterday was the best day of my life."

"For me too."

"You want something to eat? We could order up breakfast."

"Let's ask them to leave the food by the door." She paused. "It's not like we have to be anywhere today, right?"

"Right."

They ordered breakfast and sat by the window and watched the passing scene.

"Just think, we don't have to say good night at the door anymore," she said. "Isn't that a relief? It was so hard to leave you at night the past few weeks."

"Now all that is over."

A few minutes later their food was delivered. Shane, still in pajamas, opened the door and scooped up the tray just as Michelle closed the door, leaving him stranded in the hall. He knocked on the door.

"Who is it?" she called out.

"Very funny."

"I can't come to the door now. Just leave your name and address and I'll get back to you."

Down the hall a man carrying a briefcase left his room and came toward Shane.

Shane decided to make the best of it. Still holding the tray of food, he cleared his throat and, in as dignified a voice as one can muster while standing in a hotel hallway in one's pajamas, said, "Good morning."

The man chuckled. "Yes, I'd say so." He passed by.

In a loud whisper, Shane hissed through the door, "Michelle, let me in! There's people out here."

She opened the door a crack and, in the kind of western accent only managers of western tourist facilities ever use, said, "Sir, there's decent folks in this here hotel and they don't much appreciate people like you carrying on so. I don't mind telling you that we've had some complaints. So if you could just kind of tone it down, we here at Mule Creek Junction would surely appreciate it. And another thing, what on earth are you doing out in the hall in only your PJs? Come right in here this instant."

He hurried in and closed the door after him. He put the tray on a table. "Maybe you'd like to see what it's like out there, hey?" He started pulling her toward the door.

"Shane, don't . . . Shane . . . stop it . . . I absolutely can't go out like this." She pointed her finger at him the way teachers do in front of an unruly class. "If you want to enjoy the rest of this honeymoon, I suggest you stop right now. I mean it!"

He let go of her hand. "Oh, I see — it's blackmail now, is it?"

She smiled. "Hey, whatever works."

She leaned up against him and looked at the food. "Oh, yum, this looks great. Where shall we eat our breakfast?"

"How about if we eat in bed and watch Saturday cartoons?"

"Is this some secret fantasy of yours?"

"Not really. It just seems right for a honeymoon. I mean, the rest of the world is out there rushing off somewhere, and here we are watching cartoons. Also, it's something our mothers would say we're too old to do."

"Hey, then let's do it."

They sat on the bed, their backs against the headrest, eating Mexican omelettes, bacon, and toast, drinking hot chocolate, and watching cartoons.

At eleven o'clock they decided it was time to get dressed. "We got some crumbs in the bed," she said as she brushed her hand across the bottom sheet.

"No problem, the maid'll take care of it."

"Nothing's going to bother us today, is it?"

He picked up the tray, set it out in the hall, and then came back. "What do you want to do today?"

She thought about it. "Let's go to the zoo."

By the time they were ready to leave, it was a little past noon. On their way down in the elevator, a very old couple got on. The man was bent over and frail. The woman looked like a small wind would blow her away.

"We were just married," Shane said.

They didn't hear him.

"I SAID WE WERE JUST MARRIED."

"FORTY-FIVE YEARS!" said the man, thinking Shane had asked him how long he'd been married.

"CONGRATULATIONS!" Shane answered.

The elevator reached the first floor. They couldn't get out because the couple were in their way. The man seemed confused. "THIS IS WHERE WE GET OFF," his wife said.

"FIRST FLOOR IS WHERE WE'RE GOING!" the man said.

"THIS IS THE FIRST FLOOR!"

"WHY DIDN'T YOU SAY SO?"

They started walking ever so slowly into the lobby.

"THOSE TWO YOUNG PEOPLE BACK THERE WERE JUST MARRIED," she said.

"THEY DON'T KNOW A THING," he said.

133

"I KNOW, BUT THEY'LL LEARN," she answered. "JUST LIKE WE DID."

"WHERE'S THE CAR, HONEY?" the man asked.

"WE DON'T HAVE A CAR NOW. NEITHER ONE OF US CAN DRIVE."

"I KNOW THAT."

"I KNOW YOU DO, DEAR."

Shane reached out for Michelle's hand. "That's how we'll be someday."

"I hope so."

At the zoo, they wandered around in a daze. At one point they asked an attendant where the tigers were, and he said they were standing in front of them.

"If I were an animal, I'd be a tiger," Shane said, watching a tiger watch them.

"Oh yeah? Why's that?" Michelle asked.

"They get to hunt whenever they want."

"And that's important to you, right?"

"Absolutely. Just wait till hunting season. I'll bring home a nice buck and we'll butcher it in the kitchen."

In a John Wayne imitation, she said, "Well, gosh, Buckaroo, that's sure something to look forward to, now isn't it?"

"Don't forget I'm from Big Sky Country."

"Oh, right. Montana couldn't think of anything else to brag about, so in desperation they ended up picking the sky."

"Very funny. Have you ever gone hunting before?"

"No, but if you want to take me sometime, I'll go." She smiled. "So far all the activities we've shared have been worthwhile."

He leaned over and whispered in her ear, "Especially last night, right?"

"Yes, especially last night."

They walked to another exhibit and stopped. "When I was

a teenager," she said, "I knew you were growing up some- where. Whenever I was lonely or felt left out from what other people were doing, I'd think about you. Sometimes I even talked to you. Did you ever hear me?"

He thought about it. "There were times when I had choices to make. Maybe I heard you then."

The same attendant they'd talked to before came up to them. "Excuse me. Why are you two standing in front of this cage?"

"Why shouldn't we?"

"Because it's empty."

For the first time they noticed the sign, "Exhibit closed. The iguana died."

They moved to another exhibit. "Too bad about the iguana, right?" Shane said.

"A tragedy, really. What's an iguana?"

"Don't you know anything? It's a large bird from Africa."

"No, I don't think so. I'm pretty sure people in Brazil raise them for their wool," she said.

"Who cares?"

"Not me. Aren't we having fun at the zoo?"

"Opening a can of dog food would be fun today just as long as we did it together."

They approached a hippopotamus. "Excuse me, sir," Shane said, "I'd like you to meet my wife."

The hippopotamus didn't move.

"Okay, be that way." He turned to her. "He's just sore we didn't invite him to the reception."

"He's one of your relatives, isn't he? I could tell right off— there's such a strong family resemblance."

"Oh, gosh, Michelle, you really got me that time, didn't you!"

"Yep, I sure did."

The next introduction Shane made was to a giraffe. "Hey,

Big Neck, I'd like you to meet the Old Ball and Chain." He started laughing at his own joke.

Michelle punched him in the ribs. "You're on thin ice there, Bubba."

"I love it when you call me Bubba."

She whispered in his ear. "You're my bubba."

"Aren't you glad nobody's listening to us?" he said.

She put her arms around him. "I know. I feel like I'm in a trance and nothing else is real except you and me."

"What do you want to do for lunch?" he asked.

"We could have a picnic in our room."

"Yeah, right. And we could make a tent out of the blankets by hanging them over the chairs, and pretend we were camping out. On second thought, why don't we go camping for real sometime?"

"Sounds like fun. I'll bring the gingersnaps."

He wrinkled his nose. "The gingersnaps?"

"Sure. You've got to have gingersnaps when you go camping. And you'd let me wear your leather jacket. And at night we'd sneak down to the dock and eat candy bars and talk."

"And I'd bring a blanket so we could lie down and look at the stars," he said.

"Sure, why not? Let's make sure we do it before the summer is over."

"It's a deal."

As they left the zoo, she said, "I can't keep my mind on anything but you right now. Someday we'll come back to the zoo and pay particular attention to the iguana."

"Yes, someday."

"I think that when iguanas are in their woolly phase is a particularly good time to see them," she said.

"Yes, the plumage on their tail feathers becomes quite colorful then." He got a big grin on his face. "Let's go back to the hotel and see if we can get the sauna working."

"Sauna? That's a baby iguana, right?" she said.

136

"Yes, that's right. I read it on a cereal box one time."

She threw both arms into the air. "I love being married to you!"

"Me too. It's the absolute best thing that's ever happened."

"Race you to the car, okay?" she said. Only after she'd already started running did she turn to him and say, "On your mark . . . get set . . . go."

"Cheaters never prosper!" he called out after her.

As they drove to their hotel they made up a game called "This is what an iguana is like." Actually it wasn't much of a game, but for them on that day, it really didn't matter, because now they were together at last.